What others are saying about the book:

*"***Onesimus** *is captivating. I laughed and I cried, and it was so exciting I could hardly wait to see what happened next!"*

Dale Ann Ellis, Arcadia, FL

"After reading **Onesimus** *I saw Paul and the other Disciples in an entirely different light. I really enjoyed the book"*

Mike Liles, Panama City, FL

*"***Onesimus** *is one of the most exciting novels of Biblical times that I have ever read. It will hold you spellbound until the last page."*

Pauline Daniel, Fresno, CA

"While reading **Onesimus** *I cried and I prayed! This book will be a blessing to many!"*

Mary Wood, Arcadia, Florida

"I planned to read a little every evening until I finished **Onesimus**, *but I finished it in the early hours of the first morning. It should be made into a mini-series! I plan to give this book as Christmas gifts this year.*

Edward F. Coleman, Chickasaw, AL

Onesimus
The Run-away Slave

E. E. Coleman and T. Marie Smith

Cover illustration by T. Marie Smith

WestBow Press books may be ordered through booksellers or by contacting:

WestBow Press
A Division of Thomas Nelson
1663 Liberty Drive
Bloomington, IN 47403
www.westbowpress.com
1-(866) 928-1240

ISBN: 978-1-4497-1236-5 (sc)
ISBN: 978-1-4497-1237-2 (dj)
ISBN: 978-1-4497-1238-9 (e)

Library of Congress Control Number: 2011921645

Printed in the United States of America

WestBow Press rev. date: 3/11/2011

Dedication

Ervin and Tonetta Coleman

This book is lovingly dedicated to my parents, Ervin and Tonetta Coleman, who each went to be with the Lord in 2002.

They dedicated their lives to the ministry of Jesus Christ, and taught their children to work hard, be loyal and love God, family, and country.

Daddy's years of fastidious research and the drafting of an enthralling plot for the intriguing life of '***Onesimus**, the Run-away Slave*', made it possible to write and publish this book.

Contents

Chapter One

The Stoning

My left arm throbbed as I lay motionless on my back. Finally, I forced one eyelid open and saw heavy clouds drifting past a pale moon. A few stars shone feebly in the ominous black sky.

Struggling through stabbing pain, I raised my hand and assiduously moved it across the closed eye, which seemed to be covered with a dried film. My whole face was sheathed in a parched crust. *I must have been lying here several hours*, I thought. Slowly my sluggish memory returned.

Sharp pains above my left eye reminded me that a stone had cut a deep gash, and blood oozed from a burning wound in my right leg, soaking through my clothing.

I began to wearily move my aching body. No bones seemed to be broken but I had evidently lost a lot of blood. Trying to stand, I again lost consciousness.

When I regained my senses, I was on the back of a cart. Pain pulsed through my body as the wheels bumped over a rocky road.

Was the driver friend or foe? I decided to lie still until I could identify him. Faint tinges of morning light were beginning to break across the horizon. As I tried to find a more comfortable position, the driver looked back at me.

"Ah, I see you're awake, Brother Onesimus. How do you feel?" I recognized the voice of my friend Puvah, who lived about a mile from our house.

"Sore," I answered, groaning each time the wheel hit a rock, "but glad to be alive."

"Oh, yes I'm glad, too, but many were not so blessed." Sorrow gave a strange quiver to his voice.

A great lump formed in my throat, and as the cart jostled on, the gray morning sky grew brighter. Raising myself on one elbow, I looked around. I was not familiar with the hills through which we were traveling.

Reluctantly I asked, "How many died?"

"We found five, and I won't be surprised if we lose some of the others."

We rode in silence for a while, but as the road became bumpier I could not keep from crying out. Puvah reached back and patted my shoulder. "I'm taking this rocky road because we'll leave fewer tracks, and from the looks of the sky, the wind and rain will soon blot out any telltale signs that might be left. Hopefully, no one can follow us."

"Where are we going?"

"I'm taking you to the old house in the hills where you lived many years ago."

Since the Romans were stirring up the pagans to destroy all Christians, I knew he was doing what was best. We would have to stay in hiding for a long time. When I first came to this country, Martha and I lived in that old house that her Uncle Abraham built of stone. It was situated several miles back in the hills, and all those old buildings at Abraham's camp had long since been deserted.

"It'll have to do for now, but I'm sure Martha will want to go back to our own home as soon as possible."

"We'll see," Puvah said wistfully.

Although the miles fell behind us and hills loomed ahead, I knew we would never reach the old camp before the bad weather hit. "Where's Martha?"

"The pastor took her to the old house last night."

We rode on in silence. I knew we were both reflecting on our situations. The Romans and pagans were waging deadly persecution against the church. Christians still refused to bow down to the ensigns of Rome because they represented Nero, who was proclaimed to be the god of Rome, and we could not worship any god except the Father of our Lord Jesus Christ. Nearly all Christians are peaceful and refuse to take up arms, even in self-defense. However, a few served in the Roman army feeling justified to fight in defense of their country. I had never taken a position for or against taking arms as a soldier. I left that to the conscience of the individual. Under the Law of Moses, people of God had fought to protect their homes and land. Cornelius had been among the first Gentiles to receive the Holy Ghost like the apostles did on the day of Pentecost, and he was an officer in the Roman army. I had known other soldiers who were faithful men of God, but for fear that I might offend those who did not believe in fighting, I refused to defend myself. It was an easy thing for the pagan priests to lead an angry mob to beat us down with stones.

As we bumped along, my aching heart repeated the words of our Lord's injunction to pray for those who despitefully use you. The rain began to fall, and I silently prayed.

We arrived at the little house just before dark. The wind and heavy rain caught in Martha's long hair as she ran out to meet us.

Puvah pulled the horses to a stop, and she climbed in beside me. "Oh, Onesimus," she moaned as she cradled my head in her lap. "What have they done to you?"

"I'm going to be all right, dear." I tried to sound confident as Puvah moved the cart on and stopped near the door. Sarah, our daughter-in-law, hurried out to help get me inside.

"We've had a difficult time bringing enough of our things to these mountains to make this old house a fit place to live again," Martha said as I was placed on the bed.

I had been without food for nearly two days and had lost a lot of blood. I opened my mouth to reply to her, but heard no sound. Unconsciousness had again eased my pain.

As my senses returned, I heard Martha, Sarah, and Puvah praying for me, "...And I ask for his healing, Father, in the name of your precious Son, Jesus. Amen."

The aroma of fresh soup told me why Puvah was bending over the fire that crackled brightly in the fireplace. He handed a bowl of steaming food to Martha. The warm liquid she spooned into my mouth quickly disappeared.

"I think you're better, Onesimus," Puvah remarked.

"I'm sure he is," Martha said as she placed her hand on my forehead. "What you need now is a good bath and some sleep."

"Onesimus, I must go. I want to move my family some distance back into the hills. No need to walk into trouble if we can avoid it." Puvah lifted his hand in a friendly wave.

"I understand, Brother Puvah, and I'm grateful to you for bringing me home. May God go with you."

Martha brought a bowl of warm water. The soft, warm cloth soothed my face. "Onesimus, you're badly injured." She gently cleaned my wounds. "All over your back and shoulders are bruises, and two gashes on your head are very deep."

Sarah brought clean cloths and olive oil and Martha tenderly cared for each wound. I had practiced medicine for many years, and Martha served as my nurse most of that time.

"I thought most of the people in Gubbio were our friends," she muttered. "How can they turn on you like this?"

"They're idol worshippers, Martha. They were incited by the priests."

"Were you able to recognize any of those who stoned you?"

"Oh, yes," I replied. "I've treated most of them and helped bring their little ones into the world."

"They're deceived by Satan," reasoned Sarah. "We must pray for them to be saved." I began to doze but was aware of the whispered sounds of Martha and Sarah praying for the townspeople.

I slept fitfully with nightmares of the temple priests driving me through Gubbio with the screeching mob following, beating me with sticks and casting stones. I tripped and fell as the stones rained about my head and shoulders. I must have cried out in pain, because Martha took me in her arms and said, "You've had a bad dream, dear."

Sarah handed me a cup of water. "Here, Papa, you must be thirsty."

The water was soothing to my throat, but my mind could not forget the terror in Gubbio.

"They destroyed all the copies of Paul's letter that we had taken to distribute," I said. "The priests burned them—all of them!"

"You know Jacobus and I will make more copies, and we'll still give them to the people who will accept them," Sarah promised.

"Have you heard from Jacobus?"

Martha turned a worried glance to Sarah. "We're worried about him, Onesimus. He's three days late."

"He's a smart lad, Martha. He'll get through. You mustn't worry."

"But I worry, Papa. He doesn't yet know he's going to be...well, he's going to be a father." Sarah blushed and grinned at me.

"What? I di...Sarah, why have you waited so long to tell me? That's wonderful!" I raised myself on one elbow and asked, "I'm going to be a grandfather?"

Sarah nodded. "Yes, Papa, but we felt Jacobus should be the first to know."

"We'll talk about that later," Martha said, nudging me back onto my pillow. She pressed her soft lips onto my cheek. "Onesimus, my dear husband, I'm so glad God spared you for me again."

Her gentle hands tucked my old sheepskin around my shoulders, and I slept.

About an hour after sunrise the next day Sarah awakened me. I was stiff and sore in every muscle and joint. My extensive medical experience told me that I was badly injured, and perhaps I even had internal injuries I could not treat. Not wanting to worry Martha and Sarah, I tried to be cheerful.

"You seemed to sleep a little better last night, dear." Martha sat by my bed with a bowl of gruel. "I made this with goat milk, Onesimus. I'm sure it will give you strength and help your wounds to heal."

I nodded in reply, then said, "My dear, sweet Martha, you're such a good nurse." She had baked a cake of wheat and rye and had crumbled some of the crust into the gruel. As a slave in Egypt, I was given leftovers to eat. Many times the bread was burned black so I learned to like the burned taste.

"Umm, just as I like it," I said.

She smiled. "I burned it—just for you."

Brother Hamond came to see me that morning. He was a loyal pastor who had served our church for about three years and was well loved by all the Christians.

After discussing the stoning, he said, "We'll have to have our worship services in our homes again, like we did when we first started our congregation."

"I'd like that. Somehow I feel better worshipping in our homes than in the marketplace or Jewish synagogue," I replied. "But, of course they wouldn't let us use the marketplace or synagogue now for fear of the Romans."

"Well, we worship God in our hearts, anyway," Sarah broke in. "We can worship in our homes, or under a tree or wherever."

Brother Hamond agreed "I wish all our younger people knew as much about true worship as you and Jacobus."

"We've had two of the very best teachers," Sarah smiled.

"Have you heard from Jacobus?"

The women fell silent so I answered. "There's been no word, but I'm sure he'll come home soon."

"I'm afraid he'll go back to our house and be attacked, like Papa was. How will he know we've moved up here?" As Sarah wept, Martha's comforting arms wrapped around her shoulders.

The pastor prayed with us, and then said, "Brother Onesimus, I have requested that all the church members stay in hiding as much as possible for a while, and that they come here only when necessary to bring food or supplies you'll need. The pagan spies are watching all the trails to find where you live, so don't expect company for a while. If you need anything, let Sarah slip down the mountain after dark and place our symbol at the crossroad this side of Gubbio, and one of us will come to you."

"I understand, Pastor. I'm sure God will help us manage."

"Well, it's just the three of us now," Martha said brightly, trying to be cheerful as the door closed behind Brother Hamond.

"But I wish it was the *four* of us again." Sarah walked away to pray for her husband.

That night a high fever confirmed that I was very sick. I tried to keep silent so Martha could sleep, but I began to turn and thrash about the bed.

"Oh, my dear Onesimus," Martha whispered, "please try to be still. You'll start the wounds bleeding again." Her words became vague as I drifted back into delirium, and did not know what she was saying.

Just before sunrise, my fever dropped, and sweating, I fell into a deep sleep.

I became aware of a stirring in the room, but lay still, enjoying the comfort I was experiencing. I felt my old sheepskin cuddled under my chin, and the aroma of food filled my nostrils. As Martha softly hummed a song of worship, I opened my eyes and turned onto my side. The pain in my abdomen was severe, but I tried not to let it show.

"Good morning, my busy little wife."

"Onesimus, you startled me!" She smiled. "How do you feel this morning?"

"I think I'm better, but I had a high fever during the night."

"How well I know!"

She sat on the side of my bed and handed me some fresh meat and gruel. "Eat it all," she ordered. "You need it." Bending over to kiss me she whispered, "I want you to hurry and get well." Her gentle kiss caused a flicker of pain where a stone had bruised my lip.

While I ate, Martha talked about bringing our things to the old house, memories of years gone by, her love for Christ, and our work for His cause.

Soon the bowl was empty and I lay back on my bed. The soothing drone of Martha's constant vocalizations lulled me back to sleep.

Just before sundown, Martha laid her hand on my arm. "It's time for you to eat again."

I sat up and slowly touched my bare feet to the floor, but I could not stand erect. Aware that I needed to move around a bit, I shuffled a few steps to the table, but fierce pain in my lower back and abdomen caused me to wonder if my kidneys or liver were injured. I blew a sigh of relief as I eased myself onto the old wooden bench. I realized that food was essential to get well and strong again, so I ate more than I really wanted.

"Do you think you're better, Onesimus?"

"Perhaps," I replied, "but I must be truthful. I have awful pain in my back and stomach."

"Do you think your kidney may be injured?" she asked.

I thought for a moment then said, "That is one thing I have been worrying about, Martha,"

She sighed deeply and began swirling her spoon in her food, obviously worried.

To my delight, our pastor and Brother Cain came to see us the next day.

"I can tell you're better by the smile on Martha's face," he remarked.

"Yes, I'm some better, thank the Lord!"

"Onesimus, when are you going to start that book about your life?" Cain asked.

"I see you've been talking to Martha," I said.

"Yes," he replied, "and I agree with her, Onesimus. You really must write about all the wonderful things God has done for you and the things you've done for the church."

"I'm no writer," I objected. "I'm a minister of the Gospel of Jesus Christ and a physician."

"But, Onesimus," the pastor said, "Luke was also a minister and a fine physician, and just think of the books he's written. The saints are delighted to get his writings."

"Brother Hamond," I reasoned, "you must remember that Luke was with the great apostle Paul for many years, and he was told what to write on some occasions."

"Were you not also with the apostle Paul on many occasions, and, were you not saved from sin in his prison house in Rome?"

"Yes," I agreed.

"Then write about your life–write it just like you once told me."

"I'll think about it."

"Well, Praise the Lord!" Martha rejoiced. "That's more than he's ever promised me."

A week later I was sitting under a shade tree with my pen, ink and scroll. One of the brothers in our church had made a special writing table for me. To my delight it was just the right height and the finish was smooth as silk. Martha sat on the ground beside me and leaned back against the tree trunk.

Some of my external wounds had begun to heal, making it easier for me to move, but the internal injuries seemed no better.

"I don't know where to begin," I said.

"Begin at the beginning," Martha replied, moving to a large stone beside me.

"You mean that I should tell everything—even about my years of slavery, and my terrible sins? I'd be so ashamed for people to read about that," I told her.

"It won't really be true if you don't tell it all," she said. "It must be told in its entirety in order to help others who have done terrible things. They need to understand that they, too, can be forgiven. People need to know that they can lead good, useful lives in spite of their past, just as you have."

"Well, I'll have to take time to think, and try to recall those years," I said. "It won't be easy because I don't want to make any mistakes," I told her.

Brushing my cheek with her lips, she said, "While you think, I'll go fix something to eat."

Chapter Two

Humble Beginnings

I let my mind travel as far back as I could recall and began to write.

As a small lad, I loved to sit at my mother's feet and listen to the stories she told about her life. Her name was Hagar.

She said, "Onesimus, my family was very wealthy and we had a beautiful home in Myra, a city in Lycia. That's where I was born, and I lived a wonderfully happy life. My father and mother often entertained foreign diplomats, so they sent me to the best schools where I learned Latin, Greek, and Hebrew."

"One day my father incurred the wrath of a Roman officer, and a few days later, soldiers came and killed my mother and father, burned our beautiful home, and took me captive. The officer who captured me sold me to another Roman officer who was stationed in Egypt. He was not very cruel—in fact, sometimes he seemed rather kind…but…"

Mother fell silent, studying the needlework in her lap, but I knew the story. I had heard it many times before, and have many times since.

Mother served that Roman officer until he was called back to Rome for duty. Before he moved, he sold her to a greedy, affluent Egyptian in the import-export trade. He was well known in several countries for having the healthiest and strongest slaves for sale, and they brought high prices. The despot was diabolically brutal to all his slaves. After determining that mother was strong, as well as spirited, he acquired her for the purpose of breeding strong, healthy children that would bring a high price on the slave market.

Three days after purchasing my mother, the tyrant checked her teeth and aggressively passed his rough hands over her back, arms and legs, similar to the way you would examine a horse that had been bought for breeding.

"Oh, Yes!" he exclaimed with a voracious grin. "Tonight I will send a strong, young slave to you so you can conceive a healthy child." He laughed and said greedily, "You will bring me great wealth."

Mother shrank back in horror, and without thinking, she cried, "No! That isn't right. I can't do that."

His heavy hand stunned her as it connected with her face, sending her stumbling backward and landing against the stone fence. "I'll send a mate to you and you *will* lie with him!" he ordered, emphasizing each word by jabbing his calloused finger into her chest.

Mother's hand went to her stinging face as she fought to hold back the tears, but again she shook her head.

"I could not do that, Master. It is immoral and God would not be pleased if I broke His law," she answered.

Her master crushed his fingers into her shoulders and shook her viciously. His angry eyes bulged, and his brutish face frowned in fierce fury.

"You are young and healthy," he yelled through clenched teeth. "You can bear many sons and daughters who will make strong slaves for me. I will sell them and become rich–very rich indeed! You *will* obey me!"

Again mother refused. She had been brought up in a home where moral rules were very strict.

Grabbing her by the arm, the angry tyrant dragged her across a large field that now pastured horses, to an old building on the backside of his property where he had butchered, cured and stored meat years ago. As he opened the creaking door, huge rats scurried into holes in the floor, and the stench of rotting flesh still clung to the walls. There were no windows, but as the sunlight from the open doorway lighted the room, she saw a big scorpion, his deadly tail curled over his back in a menacing pose. She recoiled, but the master tightened his grip and shoved her trembling body inside. A couple of bats fluttered across the room as the bright sunlight disturbed them.

"Just see what your God thinks of *this*," he said, bellowing a vulgar laugh. "My gods all like treasure and that is what *you* are going to give them! When you are ready to accept your mate, I'll give you some food, water and a bed, but until then, you get *nothing!* I'll teach you to obey me."

Again he poked his bony finger into her chest to emphasize his tenacity. "You'll give me healthy slaves, or you'll starve!" He slammed the heavy door and terror engulfed her as she heard the heavy wooden latch click into a locked position on the outside.

His retreating footsteps sent a mixture of fear and relief through her. She stood motionless in the empty room until her eyes became somewhat accustomed to the darkness. Remembering the holes where the rats had disappeared, she chose a spot on the opposite side of the room, then took off her apron and spread it on the repulsive floor. Sitting on it, she began the long wait.

For the next few hours she listened for the footsteps of a person, but the scurrying, scratching, and occasional squeak of a rat or other creature was the only sound she heard. She tried to sing but her voice broke as tears again began to flow. The hours gave way to days. The small crack under the door, as well as a few tiny spaces between the rough boards, through which bats entered at dawn and exited at night, was the only way she knew when a day ended and the long night ensued.

Time passed. Hunger, thirst, and dread conspired against her until her nerves convulsed with burning pain. Every time a rat moved in the room, she beat on the floor, and screamed to try to scare it away. Often she felt some kind of creature crawl over her, and hysterically, she would slap it off.

On the fourth day she heard steps, but hope died when she realized it was one of the horses that roamed the field around the old building.

She grew weaker and weaker with cold nights and hot days. Often her tongue stuck to the roof of her mouth as thirst and hunger gnawed at her. After five days of sobbing with fear and hallucinations, she believed that she would soon die.

On the seventh day Mother heard the unmistakable sound of footsteps. Struggling to stand on her weak, trembling legs, her heart pounded with hope and fear. As her master flung the door open, the bright sunlight blinded her.

"Well, woman, are you ready to obey—to accept your mate?"

Mother was too weak to reply. She felt she would surely die if left in that place one more night, so she nodded her head.

"Yes? I thought so," he laughed. "Go and bathe yourself and eat a good meal, then return to your quarters."

Mother staggered out the door and fought to keep going as she heard the crude, boorish laughter behind her. Her skull felt as though it would burst. Squinting in the bright sun, her woozy head began to whirl and she slumped to the ground. Her merciless master pulled her up by the collar and then continued to hold her up as he dragged her through the weeds and dirt toward the servant's quarters. Ruthlessly he opened the door to her tiny room and dropped her just inside, slamming the heavy door behind her. She dragged herself to the water pitcher and took a swallow, and then another before splashing her face with the cool liquid.

Another slave opened the door and set a bowl of food on the table, then left without saying a word.

Mother took as long as she dared to eat and bathe before dropping her weary body onto her pallet. By then, the sun had set. Mercifully, sleep came.

A little while later she was awakened by the touch of a man's hand on her arm. Muffling a scream, she jerked away from him.

"Don't be afraid," he said in a gentle voice. "Oh, my, you're trembling, my lady. Please don't be afraid of me. Here, sit up and let's talk. We'll be alone until after sun-up."

She sat up. "T-T-Talk about what?" she asked in a timid voice.

"We'll talk about ourselves. You tell me about your life, and I'll tell you about mine. My name is Tullius."

Mother told him the story of her wealthy family in Myra and how she had come to be a slave.

"I'm so sorry," Tullius said. "I, too, was born in Lycia, but in the extreme eastern part—in the country near the Pamphylian border. Would you believe that one of our own countrymen took me prisoner and sold me to an Egyptian? He then sold me to our present master. I, too, was well educated, but it is of no use in this atrocious state of affairs. I have served him now for about three years.

They talked until almost daylight.

"I know how you must feel about having me come to you in this manner," Tullius said. "I assure you I wouldn't bother you if I could manage somehow to escape, but we will both be flogged if you are not soon found with child."

"I know," Mother responded. "I've almost lost my mind worrying."

"Let's agree between us that we'll accept each other before God as legal mates. Since the master wants to know who sired a child, he will not send anyone else to you or make me go to another woman. Maybe if we ask God to bind us as one, we will not feel so immoral," he suggested.

He studied her face in the bright moonlight that shone through the window, and then added, "I could never find a more beautiful woman to be my wife if I searched the whole world over."

Mother was beginning to like my father, and knowing she could not escape, she agreed. This was the first time she had been treated like a human being since her capture. Tullius was indeed a kind and gentle man.

About eight months later, their master died, and for the first time since they met, Mother, who was soon to give birth to me, and Tullius were separated and sold to different masters.

"It broke my heart," Mother told me, "but I never saw him again. Son, I wish you could have known your father. He was a fine man." She thought for a moment, and then confided, "Onesimus, if I could have had a choice, I would have chosen Tullius to be my husband."

I was born while mother served this new master. When I was four years old, he too passed away. That's when Master Mamun bought us and I grew up in Alexandria.

Master Mamun was a well-known physician. He trained my mother as his nurse, and she worked hard and became a well-learned and worthy assistant for him. The education she received as a girl in Myra helped her make rapid progress in the art of healing.

Mother made sure I became well educated. By the time I was five years old, I could speak fluent Latin, Greek, and Hebrew, and by the time I was seven, I had also mastered the Egyptian language. All four tongues were used in Master Mamun's household. When I was ten, I could write in all four languages. Master Mamun had a great library full of tablets, scrolls, and sheets of papyrus sewn together. He encouraged me to read and I soon became interested in bone structure, tendons, and the art of setting bones, both animal and human.

When I was twelve, Master Mamun often let me take care of broken bones so he could give himself to other phases of his practice.

Each year, from the time I was ten until I was nineteen years old, Master Mamun sent me to the eastern desert of Egypt to spend three months with his chief shepherd, Hazlot.

The eastern desert received more rainfall than the western desert, and supported rich vegetation. Many kinds of shrubs and succulents and great patches of grass grew in abundance. By moving the sheep from pasture to pasture, they managed to thrive at a profitable rate.

I always enjoyed the time spent with that very old and wise shepherd. He taught me about herbs, succulents, and roots as medicine. I also learned self-defense, with and without weapons. Hazlot's young servant was an excellent pugilist who had traveled in several foreign countries, and Hazlot enjoyed watching his servant and me as we playfully fought around the campfire. Though careful not to break bones, we often drew blood. During the months with Hazlot, I became skilled in the art of self-defense.

"Since fist fighting is not commonly used," Hazlot told me, "you will have a good advantage if you get into a real fight."

The next year Hazlot brought in another of Master Mamun's servants who was proficient with swords and daggers. For three months that summer, every night as the campfires blazed, I studied under one of the greatest swordsmen.

For my fourteenth birthday, Master Mamun presented me with a beautiful new sword. It was a broad, double-edged weapon, the kind used by the Roman army.

I continued my studies of medicine and the art of self-defense until I was nineteen. My mother was happy in her service to Master Mamun and could do almost everything Master Mamun did as a physician.

On my nineteenth birthday, Master Mamun said, "Onesimus, when you're twenty years old, I'll give you your full freedom so you will never be sold in case something happens to me. We'll go before the magistrate, and I'll sign papers of manumission. At the same time I'll offer you a full partnership in my practice. I hope you'll accept my offer."

I bowed low in profound gratitude. "Master Mamun, words fail me. How can I express what I feel in my heart?"

"I'm getting old," he continued, "and after I'm gone, you can carry on my work."

"I'll be honored to accept your offer, Master, and I will study as I never have before so I'll be worthy to step into your place when the time comes."

"That's all I need to hear, Onesimus."

Just a few weeks later, Master Mamun died of heart failure. I was miserably disappointed.

Master Mamun's wife had grown jealous of my mother, so when my master died, she sold Mother to a man none of us knew, and sold me to a stranger from Colosse, whose name was Philemon.

For the first time in my life, I wept openly. Would I ever see my mother again? Colosse was a long way from Alexandria. Would Mother's new master be good to her? How would I get along as a real slave? I was accustomed to living almost as a free man under Master Mamun, and had been able to study, write, and come and go as I pleased, going for long rides on one of Master Mamun's fine horses. I had been treated as a son, so how would it be, serving a new master?

Chapter Three

Heading Home

Master Philemon and I boarded a ship and sailed east to Gaza. Many on the ship were going to Jerusalem, and they left the ship at Gaza and traveled the rest of the way by caravan.

While at Gaza, we took on several new passengers and much cargo. The ship was loaded more than the captain wanted to take on, but since many were Romans, and most of the cargo belonged to them, he did not refuse. The ship settled into the water nearly a foot below the safe mark.

The Captain refused to sail by Caesarea, Tyre, or Sidon for fear others might want to come aboard the already overloaded vessel. Instead he put in at Seleucia, in Syria, because many people and much cargo were to leave the ship there. While in port, the sailors made repairs to the ship and sails.

"Captain, what's our next port of call?" Master Philemon asked as we sailed away from Seleucia.

"Myra, in Lycia," the Captain replied.

"May the gods help me," I cried, not realizing I was speaking aloud.

"What's wrong, Onesimus, you look sick?" Master Philemon said.

"I feel a little sick, Master," I explained "My mother's family was very rich and lived in Myra in a beautiful home. The Romans came in and killed my grandparents, burned the house, and sold my mother into slavery. She told me many wonderful things about her…er…our family."

"I'm sorry, Onesimus," he said with sincerity. "These are troublesome times. Sometimes innocent people suffer more than the guilty. That is the way in most wars."

The disinterested captain walked away to give commands to some of the sailors. I turned and leaned on the rails. Watching the waves, I tried to forget all the trouble my dear mother had gone through. As I stood there, I made a vow to the gods and to my mother that some day, some way, I would find her and take her out of slavery.

When we left Seleucia, we ran into a bad storm that lasted two days and nights. At times I felt that the ship would be lost in the gigantic waves. I became so seasick I wanted to die.

Due to the storm's having blown us off-course, we arrived at the port of Myra two days late and had to stay there three extra days while the sailors repaired the ship and sails.

"Onesimus, would you like to go ashore and see the city?" my master asked.

"No, Master," I replied, "unless you need me on shore."

He did not need me so I remained on ship. I walked along the deck and swore repeatedly that I would go back to Egypt and take my mother out of slavery or I would die in the effort. Walking alone on the deck, I looked at the other ships in port. Later that evening, Master Philemon returned. He almost ran up the plank to the deck where I was resting on a coil of rope.

"Onesimus," he exclaimed, "I've purchased the most wonderful horse in the entire world. I've seen many great horses, but this one is the greatest! He is a full-blooded Arabian stallion. You must go with me in the morning to see him."

"Very good, Master," I replied, catching his excitement. "I'll be delighted to see him. I, too, have seen some magnificent horses in Egypt. I love beautiful horses."

I slept little that night. I had only gotten a glimpse of the man who purchased my mother from Master Mamun's widow, but I judged him to be a mean man. *Mother, who had served humanity so well, was now a common slave to a tyrant,* I thought, but I finally slept.

We left the ship at dawn the next morning and ate breakfast at a little roadside shelter. A pleasant man and his wife prepared a delectable meal.

After breakfast, we swiftly walked to the pens where the horses were kept.

"Just wait until you see my new horse!" my master beamed.

I smelled the horses before we turned a corner and saw the pens. Several beautiful horses were there, but one stood like a king, his neck arched and ears pointed at us as if he understood that my master was now *his* master. He strutted back and forth in true Arabian style, dancing playfully as we approached.

The master took hold of the hackamore and the great horse snorted loudly, pawing the ground with strong, deft strokes. Master Philemon spoke with kind firmness as he reached up to stroke the mighty stallion's nose. The stable-keeper brought a saddle and bridle and put them on the horse. As Master Philemon led his beautiful new animal out of the stall he spoke to the stable-keeper in fluent Hebrew. As he had only spoken to me in Arabic, I was rather surprised.

"I didn't know you speak Hebrew, Master," I remarked in Hebrew as he fastened the girth.

He looked at me for a moment with a strange expression. "I was not aware that you did either. Where did you learn it?"

"I studied under Master Mamun, the well-known physician, for about fifteen years," I answered. "I also speak Latin and Greek."

"I am Hebrew, and it took me several years to learn Latin and Arabic. I travel a great deal and it's necessary that I speak more than my native tongue."

With that we both fell silent as he led the shiny horse from the stables. Turning to me he declared, "I think I've made a very wise purchase."

"I'm sure you have, Master," I replied "That is indeed a great animal."

"I was not referring to the horse, Onesimus. You seem well educated."

Not knowing how to respond to such a compliment, I gave a faint smile and kept silent.

He continued, "You'll be of great service to me."

"I'll do my best, Master."

"Take the horse, lead him around and get acquainted with him. Make friends with him and ride if you'd like. I'll return to the ship and get a refund for the balance of our passage and have our things brought here. We'll go overland to my home in Colosse."

Trying not to show my great excitement, I bowed low. "Very well, Master."

I took the reins and led the horse in a circle around a big tree, pleased to be trusted with such a special and valuable animal. It would have been so easy for me to mount the mighty horse and escape. I was sure no one could catch me if I were riding that great stallion, but I didn't feel this was the right time to try to escape. If I were to free my mother, I would also need money. All the money I had saved from gifts from Master Mamun, his wife had taken after he died. She even took the Roman sword he had given to me for my birthday. Yes, I would wait until I was better prepared to attempt such a venture.

I lightly stroked the horse across the forehead then rubbed his smooth neck, talking gently. Placing my foot in the stirrup, I swung onto the saddle. My mind went back to the many pleasant hours spent with Hazlot, riding horses in the Egyptian deserts, but I had never been seated so high. This was the tallest horse I had ever seen.

The stallion wanted to run, but I held a tight rein. He pranced off in a high-stepping trot. Slowly, I eased the reins to allow him a little more speed. His long legs covered the ground swiftly and I knew he could travel many miles a day. I glanced at the ground and shuddered to think what might happen if I were to be thrown.

I let the reins go slack and that horse bounded into a very fast run. I would have been sitting in the dust if I had not held fast with both hands. I managed to straighten up and felt the air rushing past my ears, and the ground was moving beneath me as if I were flying.

Too late I saw that the trail dead-ended at a wooden fence. Before I could think what to do, the charger flew effortlessly over it. I drew rein and brought him to a standstill, but by then, we were in a huge pasture where many sheep had been grazing. Now scattered by our sudden invasion, they disappeared over a little hill.

I looked for a gate, but found none. I did not know how soon my master would return and expect to find me near the stables. Deciding that I would go back the same way I had come, I turned the big red stallion toward the fence, slackened the reins, and lightly kicked my heels into his sides. He stretched into a fast run, but this time I was prepared. He went back over the fence with several inches to spare. I let him run to the big tree where I was to wait, and staked him on the green grass to wait for Master Philemon.

"Did you have a nice ride, Onesimus?"

"I did indeed, Master."

Before either of us could speak again, an elderly gentleman, accompanied by a younger one hurried toward us.

The younger man approached me. “Is this the cur that jumped his horse over our fence and scattered the sheep, Pa?”

“That’s the one!” shouted the older man, violently shaking his fist at me.

The young man took a step toward me as if to attack.

“Wait!” Philemon’s voice rang with authority. “This is my horse and my servant. What has he done?”

Expressing my regret that the sheep had been scattered, I quickly explained what had happened. “But, Master,” I added, “no harm was done—no sheep were hurt and the horse’s feet did not even touch the fence.”

“But you scattered our sheep!” the old man shouted. “It’ll take forever for us to get them back on good grazing land.”

“That’s right,” said the young man, taking another step toward me. I think he needs a good thrashing so he’ll learn to keep his mount under control.”

Master Philemon started to speak, but changed his mind when I turned to face the young man. “Come on,” I invited. “Let’s see if this cur can bite!”

I was wide across the shoulders and though my hips were not exactly narrow they were all muscle. I stood six feet and three inches in my sandals, and weighed about one hundred and ninety pounds. My fists were hardened from punching leather bags filled with small gravel, and Hazlot had trained me well to be quick with my hands.

The young shepherd stood over six feet and his arms seemed to be a little longer than mine. He probably weighed at least fifteen pounds more than I.

He came in fast and landed a wicked blow to my belly that almost took my breath. I knew by that first punch that I would have my hands full. I stepped to one side as he rushed at me the second time, so he failed to land the punch. I struck him a good blow in the ribs, but he did not seem to be hurt. He smiled and rushed me again, appearing eager to get on with the fight. The two older men stood quietly watching as we each landed several blows to the body.

Suddenly he stepped back, hung his arms by his side, and appeared to be quitting the fight. When I dropped my guard, he sprang at me like a tiger and landed a vicious blow to my face, splitting my nose and spattering blood. I went to my knees and came very close to falling in the dirt. Since he had the advantage, I knew he would most likely try to kick me, so I fell to the ground, rolled over and came up facing him.

"Can the cur bite?" he asked with contempt as he rushed in again. This time I met his rush and the training from Hazlot stood me in good stead. I struck down his defense and landed a powerful blow to his chin. I heard a snap and then grinding of bone, followed by his scream, and I knew I had broken his jawbone. His mouth flopped open and his jaw hung at a crazy tilt. His face was ashen as he sank to his knees. He looked up at me with dazed eyes before falling on his face in the dirt.

Master Philemon and the old man came closer to see what had happened.

"I think I broke his jawbone," I explained "The pain caused him to faint. He needs a physician."

"It's many miles to the nearest physician," said his distraught father. "What can we do?"

"If you'll allow me to help, I can set his jawbone," I offered. "I worked with Doctor Mamun in Egypt for about twelve years."

The boy's father and Master Philemon consented, so I went to work and soon had the jawbone back in place. I used an old saddle blanket for padding and binding, and though it smelled of horse sweat, it served the purpose. I tightened it over his head and under his chin so it could not drop out of place.

"You must be very careful," I told his father, "that he takes in only liquids for at least five weeks, and he must use a reed to drink. After that, remove the bandages and feed him only soft food until he is able to chew again. He's young and healthy and I'm sure he will heal quickly."

The groaning man regained his senses.

"That last punch broke your jawbone," I told him. "I've fixed you up and you'll be well in a few weeks."

"Thank you," the father mumbled as he helped his son walk away.

I went to the horse trough to wash the blood from my face and hands and to straighten my nose which had been knocked to one side.

Master Philemon walked up beside me.

"He nearly whipped me," I said.

"You continue to amaze me, Onesimus. If I had been told all this instead of seeing it, I probably would not believe it."

Without replying, I dried my face on a piece of old saddle blanket and waited.

"Onesimus!" Martha rushed toward me, forcing my mind back to the present. "Jacobus is home." As she threw her arms around me, a drop of ink fell from my pen, spattering the table.

"Thank God he's safe." With a happy grin I stood but could not fully straighten. Hours of writing had tired me, and suddenly I was desperate for rest. Martha slipped her hand into mine as we walked back to the old house.

Jacobus hurried to me. "Papa, it's so good to see you."

The room was pungent with cooking odors. "Thank God you're safe, son," I said with a big hug. "How did your work go? Were there any problems?"

"The Christians were excited to get copies of Brother Luke's letters," he answered, "but coming home, when I was just outside of Gubbio I heard a lot of shouting and saw the priests inciting a mob, so I had to go around the city. I hid and waited for darkness so I don't think I was seen.

"Papa," he said as he sat beside me to eat, "I'm happy to know that you're writing your life's story. I know it will be a blessing to all who read it."

"I hope so, son."

"And I believe it will be read by many people," smiled Martha.

I slept little that night. My insides were in great pain but I could do nothing for it. Just before sleep overtook me I prayed, "Father, please give me the strength to finish my book."

At dawn the next morning, Puvah and our pastor awakened me.

Puvah's voice sounded urgent. "Oh, Brother Onesimus, some of the spies sent out by the temple priests followed Jacobus home last night and…"

And they're gathering to come here," the pastor interrupted. "Brother Onesimus, they want you dead!"

Martha's hand flew to her mouth to muffle a cry.

"Quickly, Jacobus," ordered Puvah, "Let's start loading everything."

Soon our meager belongings were loaded and Puvah took us to a cave high in the mountains.

I rested for three days while Martha, Sarah, and Jacobus settled us into the cave. Jacobus found a comfortable spot for my table. I glanced back to the last lines I had written. *"Without replying, I dried my face on a piece of old saddle blanket and waited,"* I read aloud.

I chuckled to myself, "That young shepherd almost whipped me!"

As I picked up my pen, my mind quickly returned to my early years.

After I'd finished washing the blood from my face and trying to straighten my very sore nose, Philemon said, "I'll have to buy a horse for you to ride home."

Returning to the stables where he had bought his great horse, the master did not like any of them. Looking through two more stables, we finally found one. It was late so he decided to spend the night in the inn.

Early the next morning we ate a hurried meal and set out to buy a camp outfit. "There's only one inn between here and home," the master said. "We'll have to have good ground spreads because it gets cold in those mountains."

He purchased two very large blankets made of several sheepskins sewn together. They were well tanned with all the wool still on them and made the best beds one could desire.

"I'm very proud of this," I told him "Thank you. It's the first blanket of this sort I've ever seen."

We moved through country that was sparsely settled, dotted with a shepherd and flock here and there. They would lift a hand or raise their staff in greeting as we passed, but we seldom spoke to them. As I wondered why, Master Philemon said, "If we stop to visit them, Onesimus, we'll lose too much time. They're lonely men and seldom get to talk with anyone, so, once they get to talking, it's hard to get away from them."

The area we passed through was wonderful to see. It was rocky but had excellent valleys with grass and water enough to take care of many sheep.

There were no actual roads through part of the country, so we followed cattle or sheep trails. We crossed or rode down many huge canyons with walls reaching up to fifty feet in places, using trails made by wild animals. It was all new and interesting to me since I had always loved the land. We camped in a beautiful spot near a cold spring that night, and ate the food that had been bought at the inn. Early the next morning, after a hasty meal, we were again on our way to my new home.

Just before dark we staked our horses near a little brook.

Master Philemon did not ask me to cook supper, but I took charge anyway because that was the way I was trained. About forty-five minutes later, I called the master to eat.

I had already learned to wait until he gave thanks to his God before we ate. I had never thanked God for food before and it all seemed strange to me. He told me that when I became a Christian, I would understand. Of course, I had no intention of ever being converted into a Christian! I had always believed that any god was good enough if one wanted to serve a god.

"That was an excellent meal, Onesimus," Master Philemon said when we had finished.

"Thank you, Master," I replied. "I've cooked for as many as fifteen men when in Egypt with Master Hazlot."

The next day we began at a rather fast pace and kept it up until the horses became tired. We stopped for some much needed rest and food.

"You're traveling faster now than you did earlier," I remarked.

"I've been gone too long already," he explained. "I've been having trouble with thieves, too. They steal my sheep, cattle, and horses, and the Roman law won't help me."

"You are a Roman citizen and the Roman law won't help you? Why?"

"I'm a freeborn Roman," he said, "but the men who steal my horses sell them to the Roman officers for about one-half the price. Then the officers sell them to the Roman army for full price, and they keep the difference. They're all getting rich at *my* expense."

"Maybe we can stop them," I offered.

After a long silence he said, "As a Christian I hate to fight, even in self-defense. I'd never rest easy if I should kill a man."

"How long have you been a Christian?" I asked.

"About seven years. There's a small congregation that meets at my house each Lord's Day. Our pastor, Brother Archippus, speaks to us and reads from the prophets or Psalms."

"I've read Moses and most of the prophets of Israel, and I've also read most of the Psalms of King David," I told him.

"I cannot understand how you, not yet twenty years old, can speak several languages and know so much. How did you do it?" he asked.

My mother was well educated before the Romans sold her into slavery. At Master Philae's home I had access to some scrolls, and it was there I learned to read. I was about four years old. Then Master Mamun bought my mother and…"

"That's amazing," was his only reply.

We traveled through very rough country. I noticed droppings from several wild animals and also noted that we were no longer seeing shepherds.

After supper that night I put my sheepskin under the lee of a big rock that offered shelter on two sides. Carefully balancing several small stones on larger ones that would be knocked off if an animal stepped across, and knowing I was a light sleeper, I rested. Hazlot had taught me well how to survive in the wild.

I lay for an hour before going to sleep. The solitude was enjoyable as it gave me time to think. Master Mamun had taught me never to waste a conscious moment. He said, "Your mind is your most distinguishing and wonderful attribute, Onesimus, so keep it occupied on useful and worthwhile thoughts."

The stars were out in profusion and seemed so near. I wondered if they really were nearer at certain times.

Often mother and I used to watch and discuss the stars.

With difficulty I forced my mind to ponder my future. *Will I ever be a free man? Will I ever fall in love and marry a beautiful woman and continue my name as other men?*

Finally, I slept.

Chapter Four

Incident at the Inn

I awakened half an hour before sunrise and went about fifty yards down a little stream so I would not waken Master Philemon. After building a small fire, I cooked the lamb we had purchased in Myra, and made gravy like my mother used to make. I spread it over the lamb pieces. Using a thin batter with honey in it, I cooked a few barley cakes and went back to call Master Philemon.

"Onesimus, it's barely sun-up and you have breakfast ready?"

"Yes, Master," I answered, "If you will, please come eat while it's still hot."

He washed in the stream then sat on a rock near the fire. He took a big bite of lamb and gravy and then the barley cakes. "Absolutely delicious! I never tasted better barley cakes," he said.

"Try the tea before it gets cold, Master."

"Tea?" he asked. "I didn't buy tea. I couldn't find it at the market."

"Try it. It's very good," I replied.

He took a sip, and then with a nod of approval, he drank some.

"It's good. What is it?"

"It's wild tea I learned to make in Egypt," I answered, not wanting to reveal Master Hazlot's secret.

We were soon in the saddle and a strange new feeling began to surface that I didn't understand.

I have been a slave all my life, I meditated. *My parents were both slaves, but I didn't even know my father. I wonder what he was like.* The further

I rode, the more I began to rebel against being a slave. *I am not a man,* I told myself. *I'm a serf, just a worm, an animal, to move at my master's command. To be a man one must be free.* I began to hate the world and its wicked system of one man's supremacy over others, simply because he had wealth and advantage.

I remembered the words of the old shepherd as we sat around the fire one night. "Onesimus, you're too well educated and needed by too many to serve just one master. Master Mamun is a wise man and I believe he will give you your freedom."

I had been disturbed by these thoughts, but it was soon forgotten. *True to the shepherd's words,* I reasoned, *Master Mamun did offer my freedom, but it was too late.*

What good is it to think about it now? I asked myself. *Will Master Philemon ever give me freedom? I doubt it, but I will be free! I'll one day go find my mother and we **will** be free.*

"You're very silent, Onesimus," Master Philemon said.

"I'm just thinking, Master."

We had ridden into a beautiful area that was not so wild and rough. Occasionally there were a few shepherds, but their flocks were much smaller. I looked far away to the northeast where a blue haze covered some mountains. The trees were taller now and the grass more abundant.

The master's great horse was moving too fast for the little mare I rode, though she was a good horse. He finally looked back, and then waited.

"What's the name of those mountains?" I asked when we caught up to him.

"These are the Taurus Mountains," he replied. Then he added, "This horse is a mighty fast one and seems to have twice the strength of an ordinary horse.

"Yes," I agreed. "He's too fast for this little mare to keep up with over a long trail."

"I'm in a hurry to get back home," Philemon said, "and I'm anxious to find out if the thieves have struck again."

He was obviously worried. Master Mamun taught me that people often grow ill from worry. Mostly we worry about things that never come to pass. He often had his patients talk to him about their worries, then he told them to go home, think only on pleasant things and fast for three days to rid their body of toxins that worry had created. I heard him tell one man to stay close to his family as he fasted and not allow himself to worry about anything. "If trouble comes, just face it with courage," he said.

It sounded right when Dr. Mamun said it, but sounded ridiculous when I thought of telling Master Philemon, so I rode in silence.

That afternoon we saw nothing, not even an antelope or wild boar. The world seemed empty. Late that afternoon I saw a small rabbit dash away to hide in the rocks as we rode by.

The master stopped an hour before sundown. "We've been riding hard, and the horses need a rest," he explained.

We filled our water bags and hung them in the wind so they would be cooler the next day. I noticed a small lake downstream from our camp and walked down to examine it. It was clear as sunlight, situated in a natural depression.

"Master Philemon," I called "May I swim?" He nodded his approvable, so by the time he got there, I had taken off my clothes and was scrubbing my body with fine white sand that covered the bottom of the lake. I swam across the little lake and back. He was still standing there looking across the lake. I backstroked the last few yards to the shore. Turning over I said, "This is relaxing, Master. Wouldn't you like to bathe?"

"No," he said as he walked back to the campsite, "I'll wait and bathe when I get home."

Soon I dressed and returned to the campsite. I performed most of the tasks like cooking, rubbing down the horses, and unrolling our beds.

Early the next day we were again in the saddle and Philemon continued to ride in worried silence.

Late that evening we came to a crossroad and turned west.

"There's an inn about five miles down this road. We'll stay there tonight."

"Very good, Master, I replied.

"I have business with the innkeeper," he added.

I made no reply.

"We're nearing our home now. We'll be there in two more days," he added.

When we reached the inn we rode to the stables, and Master Philemon took a leather bag from his saddle. He went in and I took care of our horses and packs.

The inn was almost new with rather large, well-furnished rooms, which made it appear home-like. The furniture was different from any I had ever seen, and I learned the innkeeper had made it himself.

One piece of furniture caught my eye. It was a very large cook-stove made of stone with a large flat piece of iron across the top that they used for cooking. Across the back of the big stove there was a section made entirely of clay that seemed to serve no purpose I studied it but failed to discern what its purpose could be.

I found a seat in the corner near the big stove and turned my attention to the conversation between my master and the innkeeper.

"But I have only half that much gold here," Philemon said.

"That's enough. You can pay the balance at your convenience," the innkeeper said while writing. "Now, Philemon," he said, handing him a receipt, "One more payment and that property will be yours."

"I had planned to pay it all this time," Master Philemon said, "but when I saw Onesimus for sale in Alexander, I felt drawn to him. Somehow I felt that I had to buy him, but believe me, he cost a great sum! Then I found a magnificent Arabian stallion and, well, you know my love for great horses! There went another large amount."

They laughed and the innkeeper gave Master Philemon a good-natured pat on the shoulder.

"You know I'll give you all the time you need to pay," the innkeeper replied.

After an hour or so, heavy clouds rolled in and very dark night had fallen. I was still sitting quietly beside the stove when I thought I heard the sound of footsteps. Someone was walking from the edge of the building near the window. I quietly eased out a side door and saw a man disappear around the corner of the stable. Knowing it would be useless to follow, I stood listening. Soon I heard the sound of hoof beats heading west so I went inside and reported it to Philemon and the innkeeper.

They took lamps and went outside to look for tracks and found several near the window. Obviously someone had spent some time there.

"Well," the innkeeper sighed thoughtfully, "since someone knows this gold's here, I'll have to place a guard to watch for his return. Tomorrow I'll move it to a safe place.

"Do you really expect trouble?" Philemon questioned.

"Thieves have been working this area a lot lately. I've never lost anything but I feel that I should be careful," the innkeeper said. "I have two trusted servants to stand guard so we need not worry."

His servant, Joshua was appointed to stand guard until after midnight, and then his other servant, Phillip would watch until daybreak.

After a delicious hot meal, everyone prepared to retire. I went to my room, but instead of lying on the mat intended for me, I took my sheepskin and climbed through the window. Joshua was standing near the front of the house. Keeping out of his sight, I found some thick vines that offered a safe place to sleep. I wrapped myself in my sheepskin with my ear to the ground. If a horse came within fifty yards of my position, I would awaken. I soon fell asleep, but about midnight I heard talking. Phillip was coming to relieve Joshua of the guard.

"Has anything happened yet?"

"Not a sound," replied Joshua, "not even a rat," he added and headed to the house.

Before I could go back to sleep I heard the sound of a horse walking slowly from the west. *It must be the man who was listening under the window,* I reasoned. *Now I must be careful.* I began to wonder if Joshua and Phillip were as true and trusted as the innkeeper thought them to be.

There was filtered moonlight and I was able to see perhaps thirty feet where the horse stopped. The rider dismounted, tied his mount to a tree near the road and quietly walked up to Phillip.

"You're right on time," Phillip said as the man drew near.

"I'm always on time," the rider replied. "Did you know the man who came out of the house almost caught me at the window?"

"Yes," replied Phillip with a little laugh. "He came back and told us all about it so that's why I'm standing guard."

"He's a big man. I didn't want any trouble with him."

"He's a new servant that Master Philemon bought while in Egypt. They're both asleep in the guest rooms," Phillip told him.

I slipped out of hearing range in order to move the stranger's horse to a different position, and then returned to my lookout.

"Joshua will leave the door unlocked for me and I'll go in and get the gold. I'm the only one who knows where the Master keeps it," Phillip boasted.

"Tell me," the rider said, "where does he keep it?"

"Never! Absolutely not!" Phillip replied in a course whisper. "I saw the master take some silver pieces out one day, so I know where he keeps it. You and Joshua wait near the door, and I'll get the gold and give it to you. Joshua is running away so he'll go with you. I won't leave because I have it good here, but if you fail to bring me my share of the gold, I'll find you and kill you both! You know I will," Phillip threatened.

I had heard enough to decide what action to take and crawled silently away. I took off my sandals so as not to make any noise, and then climbed back through the window into my bedroom. The inside doors were hung with heavy curtains that smelled like well-tanned animal skins. When

I heard Phillip say he had seen the master take some silver pieces out, I thought of that odd brick addition to the stove and suspected that was where the innkeeper kept his gold. Though I could not be absolutely certain, I was willing to risk all on being right. It was simply the only logical place.

As soon as I had taken a position in a closet right close to the stove, the door opened and a form slowly and silently glided into the room. I waited, but to my utter surprise he turned through another door. So, I was wrong about the stove. What should I do now? As I pondered the situation, he came silently through yet another door. I guessed then that he didn't want the other men to see him go to the stove and reveal the hiding place, so he had taken a roundabout way.

Phillip walked slowly, silently to the back of the stove. I was hidden from his view but I could see him. He had a large bag in his hand. Quickly he removed two of the bricks from the back of the stove, took out five smaller bags and placed them in the larger bag. Then he replaced the bricks and started to stand erect. I hit the back of his neck with the edge of my hand to render him unconscious, caught his limp body and eased him silently to the floor.

Hiding the heavy bag in the closet where I had stood, I walked to the door. Joshua and the stranger were standing face to face, waiting for Phillip to bring the gold. Before they realized I was not Phillip, I caught each of them by the back of the neck and brought them together with all the strength I could muster. Taking a piece of tough animal hide from my girdle, I bound them securely and dragged them into the inn, calling loudly for the innkeeper.

He bounded into the room at the same moment Master Philemon flung open the curtain where he was sleeping, causing the candle in the innkeeper's hand to flicker wildly, singeing his long white beard.

"W-wh-what is it? Wha-what's h-happening?" The innkeeper stuttered, looking at me in the candlelight. W-w-what's the m-m-matter?" He set the candle on the table. "What's wrong with these men?" he inquired, glowering down at Joshua and the rider who were both conscious but keeping very still. "And who is this stranger?"

"That's the man who stood under your window earlier tonight, the one I told you about," I explained. "He and Joshua and Phillip planned to steal the money you placed in the stove."

"Sto...how did they know the money was in the stove?" he demanded.

The innkeeper's frightened wife came in, brightening the room with an oil lamp. "Oh, my, oh, my," she shrieked, flailing her free hand in the air. "Oh, what is happening?" she asked in troubling confusion, but no one bothered to answer.

The angry innkeeper raced to the stove and jerked out the bricks to find the money missing. He ran back through the door where he had been sleeping and quickly reappeared, brandishing a broadsword. Phillip regained consciousness and stood trembling. The innkeeper ran at Phillip and if Master Philemon had not stepped between them, I think he would have killed him.

"Move," he demanded as he swerved from side to side. "Let me at him!" the innkeeper cried, drowning out the tearful pleas of "No, no, Oh no!" from his trembling wife.

"Let me go! I'll kill all three of them right now!"

We managed to get the irate innkeeper to sit at the dining table to calm him. After a moment he demanded, "Phillip, tell me what has happened here."

Phillip dropped his head and seemed unable or unwilling to speak, so I picked up the sword from the table and pressed its point against his neck. "Talk," I commanded.

"It's really Joshua who made all the plans. He wants to run away, so he got Thomas to help him, but I was the only one who knew where you kept the money." The other two men glared at him in anger.

"How did you know my hiding place?" demanded the furious innkeeper.

"I saw you take out some coins one day, Master, and I was crazy enough to tell Joshua about it so they planned to take it and they forced me to help them."

"Then you didn't know the gold I paid him tonight was in the stove?" asked Master Philemon.

"No, Master, that was just the way it happened."

"That's a lie," retorted Joshua, straining at his bonds.

"Onesimus." Master Philemon believed I would tell the truth. "What really happened?"

As I finished the account of the story, I led the innkeeper to the closet where the money was hidden. He angrily grabbed the large bag from me and rushed back to face the thieves.

"I shall hang the three of you, first thing after daylight," he yelled. "You will die with ropes around your necks and your tongues hanging out like weary antelopes after running from dogs all day!"

His wife, still holding her lamp, moaned and paced the floor, moving the shadows about the walls in bizarre patterns.

After tying the culprits and leaving them to wait for the morning hanging, everyone went back to bed.

I waited for about an hour until I was sure everyone else was asleep. Taking my knife, I slipped quietly back into the dining room. The trio sat in terror as I stood above them, knife in hand. After listening carefully for a few moments, I bent down and quickly cut their ropes.

"Get from this part of the country, and if I ever find you back here again, *I* will hang you myself."

"Yes, master," they all replied as they quietly slipped through the door.

I made sure they all left before going back to bed.

The entire household was awakened early the next morning when the innkeeper realized the thieves had escaped. He cursed and raved and waved his sword at the other scampering servants, demanding that they find the criminals.

Finally the breakfast gong sounded and he quieted down. The hot food felt good in my tired body.

I was glad when Master Philemon said, "Onesimus, prepare the horses for an early departure. We still have two days of riding."

We had ridden about a mile from the inn in silence when Master Philemon asked, "Which way did they go?"

"They took the west road, Master. I couldn't let them die with their tongues hanging out like animals."

A faint smile flickered across the master's otherwise unflappable face.

Chapter Five

Getting Acquainted

Martha came to me as the sun cast long evening shadows. "My dear Onesimus, you can't write it all in one day. Please come eat and rest some." She studied my face and said, "You're very pale, Onesimus."

"Yes," I replied, "I wasn't aware it was so late."

Sarah was beginning to show and Jacobus was strutting around telling me that I would be a grandfather in a few months. It was a delight to have them with us. Jacobus, a good shot with his bow, kept us supplied with fresh meat. We heard no more from the angry priests who had wanted to kill me because I was the leader of the followers of Jesus. Evidently they were unable to find our hide-away. With clever hands, Martha and Sarah had transformed the cave into a clean and comfortable home.

I spent a pleasant time with my family that night before falling asleep. When I awoke the sun was high in the sky.

"Martha," I called, "why did you allow me to sleep so late?"

"You were resting so well. I could tell by your loud snoring," she teased, "and I wanted you to get all the rest you could."

"I really should have been writing by now," I said as I threw my arms around my beautiful wife.

After a late but wonderful breakfast, I returned to my writing.

Leaving the inn, we rode through some beautiful country and covered mile after mile until late in the evening.

As we prepared the camp, Master Philemon said, "That stallion held his head high and his neck arched all day. He walks like a king."

"Yes, Master," I replied "He does seem proud, and he's worthy of a king. Why not call him Pharaoh after the proud kings of Egypt?

"An excellent idea," he said patting the horse's neck. I shall call you Pharaoh—so prove true to your name."

While we were eating, he asked, "What will you call your horse?"

"With your permission, Master, I'll wait until she has established some distinguishing characteristics before I name her."

Our camp was in a cozy V-shaped nook protected on two sides by high rocks. Although it was raining, I wrapped myself in my sheepskin and slept warm and dry The animal trail we followed the next morning showed signs of recent use. When animals are led or driven by man, the trails are usually fairly straight, but when made by animals alone, they usually meander from one good grazing spot to another. The trail was leading almost due north.

"Are we getting near your home?"

"Yes," he replied. "We could get there by mid-afternoon, but I plan on going by some of the camps on the way. It may be after dark when we get home.

We were riding across a wide, fertile valley when I noticed the tracks of several horses crossing our trail and heading due east toward the Troas Mountains. Master Philemon was about three horse lengths ahead of me and had not seemed to notice the tracks. I dismounted and pretended to be tightening the straps that held my camp outfit, but I was really studying the tracks. Two horses had been ridden by here, and on each side of the horses that carried riders were the tracks of another horse. That made two sets of three horses, six in all. I figured that the horses being led could have been stolen and were being taken to a holding station in the mountains. I mounted up and rode to where Philemon was waiting for me.

"Was some of your pack about to fall off?" he questioned.

"Not really," I answered "I just made it more secure."

We began to see many sheep and cattle but few horses.

"Who owns these animals?" I asked.

"They belong to different men who live between here and Colosse. I own many of them, my neighbor, Sir Galalai, owns some, and my friend, Sir Seth, owns many.

"Then this grazing land is owned cooperatively?"

"Yes," he explained, "it's free to anyone who owns animals and wants to bring them here to feed. The grass is good and there is plenty of water.

Having read many of the laws of Greeks, Romans, and Hebrews, I wanted to ask more questions but decided to wait.

As we rode, the master pointed out several houses, telling me his neighbor's names and whether or not they grazed their animals on open range.

I carefully watched for tracks of the horses that had crossed our trail earlier. I thought I saw them once, but the wind had blown them until I could not be sure. Suddenly, there they were again, plain and easy to read. I stopped and called my new master.

"Master, come back here, please. I want to show you something."

He came back. "What's the matter?"

"See, Master," I pointed out, "there are two sets of tracks. Each set was made by three horses. The horse in the middle of each set carried a rider, and the horses on each side were being led."

"Are you telling me how many horses passed by here and how many carried riders just by their tracks?" he asked.

"Yes, Master," I answered.

"Humm," he thought, "I've never heard of such a thing," he said skeptically.

"When I stopped back there, I was studying these same tracks," I said. "They crossed our trail and headed due east toward those mountains."

"How do you know those were the same tracks?"

I dismounted and motioned for him to come where I was kneeling over some well-defined hoof prints.

"See here." I took a straw and pointed to a certain track. "This track is deeply imbedded in the soil and if you will note, it has a bad nick torn out of the right side of the hoof. Riding in the rocky, mountainous country most likely caused that. I noted the same track when I saw them before."

He looked bewildered and asked, "What do you think it means?"

"Well, Master, it's my guess that you lost four more horses last night and they are now safe in the mountain where they are holding them, just waiting to be delivered to the Roman army."

"Why do you say they were stolen last night?"

"It rained very hard about midnight. These tracks were made after the rain or it would have destroyed them."

We rode on in silence. He appeared in deep thought, but finally spoke.

"If you're right and I did lose four horses last night, then I'll take three or four men and go after them."

"May I go with you, Master?"

"I wouldn't go without you."

We left the trail and rode toward a large flock of sheep. Two big dogs meandered on the periphery of the flock.

An active old shepherd stood when we rode up. "Greetings, Master Philemon. It's good to see you again," he smiled, bowing low.

"I'm glad to see you, too, Hezikah. How have you been?

"I'm well, Master, and so are the sheep. Their wool is growing heavy and it looks like there'll be many lambs this time," he replied.

"Hezikah, this is Onesimus. He'll be staying with us now. I'm proud to have him."

"Greetings, Onesimus." The old shepherd smiled. "You'll be happy as we all are to serve our good master."

Remembering I had said the same thing about Master Mamun, I nodded and smiled.

"Now, Hezikah, tell the bad news," Philemon said.

A serious frown creased the old sheepherder's leathery face. "Master, bad news it is, but I can't keep it from you. Late last night we were all asleep, and just after the hard downpour two riders came into your herd of horses and rode away. It was too dark to follow.

"Did anyone try?"

"No, Master," was the reply "It was very dark."

'Which ones did they steal?"

"Three of your best mares and that big black stallion you bought from Master Galalai."

"Well," said Philemon, "the Lord giveth and the Lord taketh away. Blessed be the name of the Lord."

"Amen," said the old shepherd reverently. "We're all very sorry, Master."

"Hezikah, is there anything you need from the big house?" I soon learned that the house where the servants slept, ate, and kept food supplies was called 'the big house.' It consisted of many rooms.

"I guess not, Master, unless you want to send me a bit of meat. I'm full up to here with barley cakes and honey." He patted the top of his head and a wide grin broke out on his face.

"I'll see that it's sent to your camp the first thing in the morning," Philemon assured him.

We turned our mounts to the corral, about four acres of fine grass with a spring bubbling up in the center, creating a small stream. A rock wall formed two sides of the pasture, but the other two were flimsy wood and stone, carelessly thrown together. Man or horse could come and go with little effort. The lush grass and water is what kept them there.

"Until about four years ago, we never thought of fencing our livestock. Then the Roman army began buying cattle for food and horses for war, and we began to lose our stock," Philemon explained.

"I can sympathize with you," I said as I remembered how I lost my cherished sword.

"Master, do you have a bow?"

"Why a bow?"

"It's a rather efficient way to protect yourself," I tried to explain, "and, if we're going after those horses, we'll need powerful and silent weapons."

"I'm sorry, Onesimus, but I don't own one," he said, "but each man will have a spear and a sword."

"I trust I may have a short Roman sword and a good mace," I requested.

"I prefer the long keen-bladed swords like King David chose to arm his army," he stated.

"Master," I stated, "I believe the heavy Roman blade is better in close combat because it will often cut through a habergeon, or other body armor."

We rode on in silence but I could see my master was displeased with my remarks.

We rode toward the horse camp, stopping to enjoy the cool spring water before riding on.

"Hail, Master," yelled a young man about twenty-three years old—tall, tanned, and well built. He was neatly dressed in a tight-fitting garment as was worn by the Roman soldiers. A frown creased his otherwise friendly face.

"I'm ashamed, Master," he said "I was absent when the thieves came. They took four of your best horses."

"Well, John, they seem to know the best time to strike," answered Master Philemon.

Cephas, John's father, came out of the camp tent and hobbled up to where we sat in our saddles. He was obviously in pain.

"Greetings, Master," he said in a low voice.

"It's good to see you, Cephas," the master said. "I'm glad to know you two are all right."

"My old joints won't let me move like I did a few years back," the old wrangler said.

"Well, I've been thinking about you, Cephas," Philemon said "I've decided you are to move to the big house. Your only task will be to keep the water jars on the porches full from morning till night. The rest of the time will be yours."

The old man's face lit up and his eyes filled with tears. "That sounds good, Master. It's been good to serve you all these years." His voice began to tremble. "I-I don't know if I can make it without a regular job."

"You've earned it, Cephas. You were serving my father when I was born," Philemon remembered.

"Cephas, this is Onesimus," he said, nodding toward me. "I brought him from Egypt." I raised my hand as they both welcomed me.

"John, tell me about the horses."

"Master, I had gone to the big house for supplies and that storm came up suddenly. I stayed there until the rain stopped and got back here after midnight. Father told me about it, but it was much too dark to follow them. I'm sorry, Master."

"I don't blame you for the loss, John, but I want you and Onesimus to help me find them. I'm tired of this horse stealing."

"Thank you, Master," John answered.

"I wish this old leg would let me go, Master, but I'd only be in the way," Cephas said.

"John," Philemon continued, "I want five saddle mounts and two pack horses here by mid-morning."

"They'll be ready, Master," John called as we rode toward the house.

We rode into the yard of the big house and many smiling servants ran out, waving their hands in happy greeting. It was evident they loved their master.

"Elias," Philemon said, "this is Onesimus. He's one of us now so assign him a good place to sleep, and a place at the table. He's going with me on a big task tomorrow."

Master Philemon rode on to the yard at his house and handed the reins to a young lad who led Pharaoh to the stable.

"Well, Onesimus, don't just sit there all night," Elias called and then motioned for a lad to take my mount. I removed my packs from her and walked to old Elias. He looked me over much as one would an animal he was about to buy. The old servant drew himself as straight as he could and looked up into my eyes. "Time was I stood as tall as you. Time will be when you stand as I now stand, so keep your pride underfoot and we'll get along just fine. Come on in, Onesimus, and welcome." He patted my back and grinned.

I loved the old man from the start and learned that he was the oldest of Philemon's servants. Elias gave the orders to cooks, waiters, house cleaners, and yard laborers He also handled purchases and disbursements, as well as the blacksmith, tool, and saddle shops. He was responsible for clothing, sandals, and other items for the many servants under his care.

He was a father to all, a man who had grown wise with age and knew how to command respect and obedience without ever demanding them. I had never known my real father and before many days, I had come to think of Elias as a father. I sometimes wished my mother could meet this grand old gentleman.

Elias had served Philemon's father for many years and was well read, speaking Greek and Hebrew as well as I. Hebrew was the tongue used in the household most of the time.

John came early the next morning, leading the saddle mounts and packhorses. Master Philemon joined us about mid-morning and soon we were in the saddles.

Our search party consisted of Master Philemon, a servant named Rabbath, Seth – a friend who who recently lost horses to thieves, John and me.

Somewhere, Elias had found a short, double-edged Roman sword that he handed to me just before we rode away. I smiled my appreciation to Philemon and he returned it with a nod. All the others were armed with graceful and efficient Damascus type swords. They reflected scintillating rays of sunlight that could be easily seen from a long distance. I knew we could never get close to the thieves in the daytime without their seeing us, but I said nothing. I still preferred my rusty old Roman weapon because it could be used as a mace to crack heads or break arms if we got into a battle.

I had never been in a real battle, but had seen one in Egypt when I was about eight years old. Seven Egyptians defeated eleven thieves who were trying to steal the royal treasures. The soldiers with their Roman swords won easily over the thieves with long flashing blades.

We rode out at a fast trot that we maintained for about eight miles before Philemon came to a halt.

"Now men," he began as we gathered around him, "I know Onesimus is young, but he has been trained to track men and animals. If the horses can be tracked, I believe he can do it, so you go ahead and find the tracks and we'll follow."

Touching my heel to my mount, I rode out ahead and set the pace, knowing we would need rested horses when we located the thieves.

We wasted no time, but rode cautiously until we came to the place where I had seen the last set of tracks. I dismounted and studied the prints and again I noticed a chipped place in one of the hooves.

"What's he doing now," Seth asked.

"I don't know but he knows how to track so I'll leave it to him."

We mounted and rode east-southeast. I knew that we would cross their tracks again a few miles up the trail if they were headed for the mountains. The first set of tracks I had seen yesterday went toward the east, so I rode about two miles then waited for the men.

"Sirs, I want you to search for horse tracks going east. If you find any, please call it to my attention."

The grass was high and the wind blew hard and I knew that most of the signs would be destroyed. When we had ridden another mile I decided we had failed to find the tracks because we should have crossed them before now. I waited for the men to catch up.

"I'm sure we rode past the tracks, Master Philemon. With your permission you and the men can stay here and I'll search for them alone for a short while."

Philemon nodded.

I rode south for about half a mile then rode in a great circle, searching carefully. Finally, there they were, so I followed them for a short distance until I found some soft earth. Dismounting, I found the track with the chipped hoof and then rode back to the others and waved for them to join me.

When they rode up I said, "See, Master, this is the same track I pointed out to you yesterday We're on the right trail now."

"Very good, Onesimus," said Philemon.

"Master, I'm sure the thieves will have a guard on duty. I suggest that we follow the trail a few more miles, and then find a depression where we can rest until after dark so we can slip into the mountains and find their campfires."

"Sounds good to me," Seth offered.

We rode slowly for about three more miles before making camp, then prepared a meal and waited for darkness.

After sleeping an hour, we silently rode due east into the mountains. Not wanting to ride into an ambush, we had chosen a very high mountain peak that stood out against the star-studded sky to use as a landmark, and then moved cautiously into the timbered slopes looking for campfires. We rode about another mile and a half before we saw firelight.

Philemon signaled a halt. "What kind of attack do you suggest, Onesimus?"

"Well, Master, let's move on very quietly until we can see some of their men before we make our plans," I whispered.

"Very well," he agreed. "Ride on men."

The fire was further than we thought, and when we could see the men, we were deep in the mountains. Master Philemon stopped and we gathered around him.

"All this is new to me," he admitted. "Do any of you have advice to give?" Everyone stood silently watching the flickering fire for a few seconds. When no one spoke, Philemon asked, "Onesimus, what do you suggest?"

Speaking softly I said, "I think we should leave one man with the horses, Master, while the rest of us go as near as possible without being seen. If we can locate the horses and stampede them, they'll go back to their home range without our driving them. We might not have to fight."

All the men nodded in agreement.

We advanced cautiously until we heard the thieves talking. After listening a few moments I volunteered to go in and stampede the horses. When the master agreed, I crawled past the camp on the north side where there were at least thirty horses fastened to a rope that had been tied between two trees about fifty feet apart.

The thieves had chosen a very narrow pass for their campsite, just wide enough to build a fire and sit comfortably around it. Four men were eating and talking around the fire, and three others, wrapped in their blankets, seemed to be asleep. There was another path around the outside of a huge rock that sheltered the camp. *The horses will take the outside path and stay clear of the campfire,* I thought. *Then we can drive them to our ranges without confrontation. They'll never catch us on foot.*

I eased up behind one of the trees, which secured the rope, drew my knife and with one quick slash the horses were free. I yelled as loudly as I could and struck a big black stallion on the rump. They all bolted, but to my amazement headed straight for the campsite in a mad stampede.

My hands flew to my temples as though they automatically triggered my mouth to drop wide open and issue a groan of hopelessness. I stood powerless and watched them run ferociously through the camp. The men who were awake tried to dash for safety, but two of them were knocked down and trampled under flying hooves. The three sleeping men had no chance to escape and were crushed by the crazed horses.

The horses disappeared into the darkness just as Philemon and the others came running into camp. We found four men dead and another so badly wounded that he soon died. I made a quick mental note that two had escaped.

"Let's camp here the rest of the night," suggested Seth.

"That sounds good. In the morning, will you see to the burying, Seth?" requested Philemon. "Rabbath, stay here and help Sir Seth. John, you and Onesimus see to our horses."

Early the next morning, a very distressed Philemon turned Pharaoh toward home.

A few days later I asked Elias why the master did not eat nor come to give orders.

"The master is a Christian," he explained, "and he's deeply hurt and feels guilty because those men died in the stampede. Master Philemon is fasting."

"But it was better for the horses to kill them than for us to engage in battle and kill some of them or be killed," I argued.

"Yes, I agree, but the master said he would rather lose all his horses than have one man die in order to save them." Elias' tone was somber.

I sat quietly trying to understand. I had been trained to do what was necessary to protect your own property, and never have a second thought if a thief was killed. Unable to understand, I changed the subject.

"What would you like for me to do?" I asked.

"Master Philemon asked me to have you take care of Pharaoh. Ride him every day and give him a good workout once or twice a week. See that he is fed well and rubbed down after each ride."

"That's one task I'll dearly love," I said happily.

"He also told me that you are to move to the room above Pharaoh's stall. There's a table, plenty of candles, and everything you'll need to be comfortable, including another thick skin for your bed. You'll continue to come to the big house for meals."

"Very well," I said "With your consent I'll take my things there now."

I sat on a stool beside the table and began to think. Thoughts can be more harmful than weapons. Good thoughts promote well-being in the spirit, but wrong thoughts can leave lifelong scars on a man. The thoughts I was thinking were not good. Thoughts of my mother made me sad. I thought about the years that my mother and Master Mamun spent to give me the best possible education. I also realized that that knowledge placed tremendous responsibility on me. I wept as I remembered the words of the old shepherd Hazlot, telling me someday I would be free.

But here I am, I thought, *in a strange land, among these abominable Christians who weep over the death of a thief yet bind me here to serve a horse instead of the people I've spent my life preparing to serve. I swore to the gods that I would get my mother out of bondage, but, of course, to do that I'll have to run away. Oh, I almost wish I were a fool, unable to read or understand any other science.*

The supper gong sounded so I washed my face and went to the big house.

Some time later I spoke to Philemon. "That was a wonderful day when Master Mamun bought my mother and me. It gave me a chance to become educated under a master."

Philemon gave a disinterested nod.

I took a deep breath and pursued my line of thought. "Master Mamun and Hazlot agreed."

After a moment of silence he asked, "Agreed on what?"

"They agreed that I had the ability to become a great physician and that I should have my liberty to pursue my calling. Master Mamun had promised me a writ of manumission but he died before he could give it to me."

Philemon gazed at me in solemn thought. Finally he turned his gaze toward the mountains, folded his arms and said with quiet control, "Onesimus, you belong to me. I paid a great price for you, and you'll use your wisdom and healing touch here—among my household."

"Master, please," I begged "Allow me to make an offer. Let me go to Colosse or even Ephesus and open an office. I'll repay you all that you paid for me and more."

Philemon listened to my request, looked me in the eye and smiled, then walked away without replying.

I watched him disappear into the house. My malignant thoughts tormented my mind allowing hatred to flourish. I recalled that the innkeeper had not even said 'thank you' when I saved all that gold for him. I was only a slave—why should he thank me? And I was sure that without my help, Philemon would never have gotten his horses back, but he expressed no thanks. *I'm his slave,* I thought bitterly. *I owe him all this.*

For the next year I served as conscientiously as possible, caring for Philemon's family, servants, and animals. I enjoyed the work and no one realized that bitter anger burned within me, but often I reaffirmed my vow to find Mother.

After lunch one day I saddled the great horse. As soon as the house was no longer in sight, I let the reins go slack, touched his flanks with my heels, and gave a Saracen yell. I let Pharaoh run—and that horse could run! I headed north as fast as he could go.

A caravan road ran about three miles north of Philemon's place. When I got close to the road, I saw several cooking fires and headed Pharaoh in that direction. I noticed the wheelwright at work repairing a broken wheel, but since I know very little about wheels, I offered no help. It looked as though one of the wagons had been overloaded. Some made camp and were cooking while it was being repaired. I soon learned they were traveling from Lystra to Ephesus. I rode slowly down the entire length of the twenty-four-wagon caravan. There were also about fifteen mounted men, and sixteen or more Roman soldiers riding with them to protect them from highwaymen and others who were a danger.

Many happy children were running and playing, very glad to get out of the cramped wagons.

I studied the people, the animals, the soldiers and their armor. Various carts and wagons told me they were from many parts of the country to the east. Riding back up the other side of the caravan I greeted several people who gave me close scrutiny, but Pharaoh got the most attention. The mounted men motioned and talked about him as I rode by. Even the soldiers stopped to look with greedy eyes at the great horse.

I noticed someone sitting in one of the wagons with her back to me. Just as I came abreast of her, she turned and we looked directly into each other's eyes.

I'd seen some extremely beautiful women in Egypt, but I had never seen anyone as radiantly lovely as this girl. I pulled Pharaoh to an abrupt stop and gazed at her in silence. Hypnotized by her eyes, I sat there numb, speechless and getting more embarrassed by the minute. She smiled and my heart began to pound. I wanted to speak to her, to tell her that she was the exact fulfillment of my dreams—that she was the woman I would want to marry but the words froze on my lips.

I became conscious of a low murmur and looked around. Several older women were talking and snickering about my obvious confusion. I felt the blood rush to my face, even down my neck, and knew I was blushing. I had seen several young ladies blush when they met young gentlemen, but this was different. She seemed so perfectly composed!

I was about to jab my heel into Pharaoh to escape when a little boy fell out of the next wagon. I knew by his scream that he was badly hurt. Immediately composure replaced confusion, as I knew exactly what to do. I tied the reins to a wagon wheel and rushed to the child. His terrified mother, unable to hush the wailing looked at me with pleading eyes.

"I'm a physician," I told her. "Let me have him."

I placed him on a blanket spread in the shade of a tree and quickly found that his arm was broken. I asked for straight sticks for splints, clean cloth and olive oil. In a few minutes the arm was tightly bound and placed in a sling. I gave the snubbing but smiling boy back to his mother, who thanked me and offered a piece of silver for my services.

"No," I replied "I hope to set up a physician's office in Ephesus some day. Maybe I can be of service to you again."

I bowed low to the mother and gave the child a pat. As I turned to mount Pharaoh, there was that girl again, standing with her hand on Pharaoh's forehead. He held his head down in order for her to reach.

"We're all thankful for your helping my little cousin," she said with a smile. Her voice was soft and velvety.

Again I was at a loss for words. "I was glad to be of help," I managed to say.

My mother had taught me that I should know the girl to whom I gave my heart. She said there was no such thing as love at first sight. What were these feelings that were rushing into my heart? I knew nothing about this girl. Can I possibly be in love with a stranger, I wondered.

"My name is Martha," she finally said.

"And my name is Onesimus," I returned, fumbling with the reins which I had untied from the wagon wheel. Having regained some self-control, I said, "Where are you going, Martha? I must see you again."

"I'll stay in Ephesus with my aunt for a few weeks, and then I'll make my home with my Uncle Abraham in Rome."

"What part of Rome?" I asked. "It's a very large city." We began to walk away from the others.

"Since I've never been to Rome, I can't tell you," she shrugged.

"I'll find you anyway," I declared. "Just you wait and see!"

She stopped momentarily, lifted her eyebrows and smiled a quizzical half-smile.

"But why should you find me?" she questioned. "We've only just met and we're complete strangers." We were then far enough from the caravan that no one could hear and I was more at ease.

"But I feel I've known you for a long time. When I first saw you and looked into your lovely eyes I knew that I loved you," I blurted.

"That cannot possibly be," she said with pretended indignation. "I must know and understand a man before I can tell him that I love him." Her smiling eyes spoke the plain language of love and I knew that her heart was not in her words.

"I've studied all my life to become a doctor. The great Doctor Mamun in Egypt taught me for many years and I am already qualified to practice. I will open an office someday and I want you to share my life."

Shocked, she stood with a blank look on her face. For a few moments, I thought she was going to run back to the wagon, but instead she smiled, "Are you asking me, a perfect stranger to be your wife?"

"Please don't make fun of me," I begged. "I've never been more serious in all my life. I've never seen another girl that I felt so drawn to. I know that I love you."

She looked into my eyes and said, "Onesimus, I'd never make fun of you. I feel you are in earnest, but what can I say? I like you and your forthright manner, but I just can't give you an answer now. It wouldn't be proper."

"Martha," my voice trembled with emotion, "you're my heart's desire. Please promise that you'll wait for me. I assure you that I'll come to Rome and find you and get a final answer to my proposal."

A voice rang out, "Get ready to travel. We've a long way to go."

As Martha turned to walk back to her wagon, I noticed a tear in her eye.

"Will you wait?" I asked.

She nodded, then ran back and climbed onto the wagon. I jumped on Pharaoh and rode along beside her. "I'll see you again, Martha, I'm sure of that because I love you. I'll find you when the time is right."

Martha gazed at me with amazement and anticipation. "You'll find me at my Uncle Abraham's place in Rome," she called out with a smile. "He's a tentmaker," she added before she crawled quickly out of sight under the wagon covering.

I sat motionlessly on Pharaoh but my heart was pounding as though the mighty stallion was galloping through my chest. I watched the caravan move over a little hill then disappear from sight, but I knew it could be seen again when it topped the next hill. I sat and watched until it was in view, then raised my hand high in a lingering wave. Finally, a white cloth waved in response and then fell to the ground.

After a quick kick, Pharaoh was soon at the spot where the cloth had fallen. I dismounted and picked it up. It was the scarf that she had been wearing and smelled sweetly of her. I placed the lovely white scarf in my girdle and rode slowly back to the stall. After caring for Pharaoh, I climbed up to my room.

"I *will* escape somehow," I declared under my breath. "I *will* deliver my mother from slavery and find Martha. Whatever the cost, *I will do these three things!"* I promised myself.

I paced the floor over Pharaoh's stall for the rest of the afternoon trying to think of some way to get my freedom. I was now sure that there was no other woman for me as I thought about Martha's smile, her fragrance, and, oh, those beautifully breathtaking eyes. I could close my eyes and vividly see hers, and hear her say again, "You'll find me at my Uncle Abraham's place in Rome." That was almost like saying "yes" to my proposal, and she did tell me she liked me.

My thoughts were disrupted by the supper gong so I headed for the big house. I ate little and said less.

After supper Elias said, "Onesimus, you're very quiet. Are you worried about something?" His concern sounded genuine.

"Just thinking, Sir," I assured him as I started back to my room.

Life had been easy these past couple of years at Master Philemon's. I had taken care of Pharaoh and had used my healing art for Philemon's household when necessary. Elias assigned a few odd jobs when I had time to spare.

Each day I realized more that Philemon was far wealthier than I had first thought. One thing I must say is that he treated his servants like human beings and hardly ever punished them.

"Onesimus," Philemon said one day, "Get Pharaoh ready for me to ride to Colosse."

"Master, may I go also?" I asked. "I've never been to Colosse." He nodded so I saddled the little mare I had ridden from Myra and we were soon on the road.

While Philemon was attending his affairs, I went to the physician's office to get acquainted with him. He was old but active and had a strong voice and seemed to be well learned.

"I'm Onesimus," I introduced myself, "a servant of Master Philemon."

"I'm Doctor Joash," he replied. "Philemon is a good man."

"Yes, he is a good man." I sincerely meant it.

"What can I do for you, Onesimus? You look healthy as a young bull."

"That I am, Master Joash. I didn't come for treatment. Master Philemon had business in town and I came with him. I served under Master Mamun in Egypt for nearly fifteen years and he taught me much about the healing profession. I would like to know if you have some good books on medicine that I might borrow. I want to continue my studies.

He looked at me with a quizzical eye. "I've heard many things about Doctor Mamun. He was a well-known physician. I met him in Jerusalem about ten years ago."

"I remember when he made that trip," I said "I wanted so much to go with him, but he said I'd have to stay and help my mother take care of the patients."

"Was your mother a physician?"

"She was a trained nurse when Master Mamun bought us. He took her into his practice from the beginning, and in a short time he was able to travel and leave his patients in her care."

"Yes, Doctor Mamun was great man. I was sorry to hear about his death."

"I do have some books that you can borrow," he said after a short time of silence. "What tongue do you read?"

"I read most languages that are used today."

He handed me a book written in Latin and asked that I read a certain passage.

"I'm very surprised," he said when I had finished reading. "Most young men cannot read their native tongue, and here you read others as well.

"Master Mamun taught me to read Latin, Hebrew, Greek and Arabic."

"Really!" he exclaimed. "That's quite an accomplishment."

"I see that this book is by Joash the Physician. Is this your work?" I asked.

"No, Joash was my grandfather. I was named for him. I'm a fourth generation doctor."

"That's wonderful," I told him. "You must be very proud of your family."

"Yes, I am," he replied. Seeing his pride I smiled as he asked, "Are you going to be a doctor, too?"

"It's my greatest ambition," I said earnestly, "but I'm just a slave." I cast my gaze down to the floor.

When I looked up again he said with compassion, "Onesimus, never be ashamed of being a slave, and don't think you can't be a physician as a slave. Some of the greatest men I have ever known were in bondage." I said nothing but felt humbled. He continued, "Of course only a few slaves go on to become great men, but it would seem you might be one of the few."

"Thank you, Master Joash. Those kind words are healing to my spirit and I need that."

"I can tell that you were trained by Doctor Mamun. That sounds like his philosophy. He was a pioneer in the field of mental and spiritual remedies," Doctor Joash said.

"Yes, he was," I agreed "and I am fortunate to have trained all those years with him."

Master Philemon came in.

"Greetings, Doctor Joash. I hope Onesimus has not detained you from your work."

"No, no, Philemon. Onesimus is a fine young man and he was no trouble at all."

Philemon smiled and said, "That is true." Then turning to me he said, "It's time to go."

"Philemon," Doctor Joash walked thoughtfully to his side, "I would like for you to consider leaving Onesimus here with me for a few months so he can continue his medical studies and be my apprentice. I'll be glad to pay for his use."

"I'm afraid that will not be possible right now," he replied "I need him at my house."

"I'm getting old, Philemon, and will soon be forced to retire. There is no one in Colosse to take my place."

"It is out of the question," Philemon stated with finality then walked out.

I took the two books Joash held out to me. He offered his hand, which I took quickly in a tight grasp.

"Come back every chance you get, Onesimus. I've enjoyed talking with you."

I was overcome with emotion as I said, "Thank you, Doctor Joash."

When I mounted, that little mare tried to throw me as she had done many times before. Already frustrated, I jerked the reins tightly, forcing her head almost between her legs and cried, "There, Hebel, take me to the big house."

"Hebel?" Master Philemon laughed. "So that's the name you've chosen for her."

"Yes, Master. I just now called her that for the first time but it is a fitting name. She is vanity and vexation of spirit," I said with a frown.

With a loud laugh Philemon dug his heels into Pharaoh and he was in a run with Hebel right behind him.

"Papa," Sarah's sweet voice interrupted my writing, "Mama wants you to come in and rest for a while."

With Sarah's help I managed to stand but fell back into my chair. Though the pain was severe, I laughed and remarked, "Your old Papa's not getting around very well. Let's try it again." Before I knew it, Jacobus was behind me, tenderly helping me to stand.

My strength is failing a little more each day and I'm never without a fever. Martha has detected it and she seems to worry.

The persecution of Christians is continuing with renewed fervency so we must continue to live in the mountains. The cave is small but Martha and Sarah have made it comfortable, and about once a month an elder or the pastor comes to see if we need anything, but there are no other visitors.

"Tomorrow I'll write again," I told Sarah and slowly started toward the cave.

"How's my first grandchild?" I asked, smiling.

Sarah patted her bulging stomach. "Growing, Papa, growing."

Chapter Six

Running Away

Things usually went well on Philemon's place. Though a strict disciplinarian, Philemon was also a true gentleman. He was quick to punish deliberate disobedience and just as quick to forgive and forget, never seeming to hold a grudge or mentioning a fault from the past. Old Elias followed his example. Cephas was happy with his duty as a water boy. That kind old gentleman spent most of his time lying in the shade of the giant ferula bush that grew near the end of the porch.

I cared for Pharaoh but I rode him only when necessary for exercise. I spent most of my spare time reading the books borrowed from Doctor Joash. Doctor Mamun had taught me most of what was contained in the one written in Hebrew, but the one written by Doctor Joash was full of new information. Several pages were devoted to hot and cold baths and packs, in addition to methods I was already familiar with. I also learned that the root of the ferula bush, like the one old Cephas rested under, contained asafetida and galbanum which were helpful in treating certain breathing problems and some skin rashes.

I learned that Master Philemon had thousands of sheep, goats, horses and cattle, with shepherds and cattle herders going far and near in search of the best grass and water. He had many acres growing grain. At the end of each month, servants I'd never met before would come to the big house. There were also many hired workers who worked for a share of the animals they tended or the grain they produced. Philemon was indeed a very wealthy man!

As I saw others working and getting paid, it rankled my spirit and I daily grew more bitter. I knew my attitude was wrong but my mother called to me from across the water. I often awakened in agonizing fear for her. I also longed to go to Rome to find Martha. *Will I ever see her again? Will I ever have a family? Yes, I will find them soon.*

Wisdom and education are purveyors of burdens that less educated men never feel, I thought. *Added abilities demand more responsibility. Must I stay here all my life and care for a horse or occasionally set a broken bone for some careless slave? I'm not a criminal, but I feel the only answer is to run away.*

I'd been here over three years and read many books borrowed from Doctor Joash. I was certain that I knew more than most physicians.

My twenty-second birthday came with no mention of it from anyone. Self-pity is not good, but I made no effort to avoid it.

I made my way to the main house and asked Master Philemon if I could return some books and borrow some more.

"Not now," he replied. "Wait until I need something from Colosse."

Three weeks later John and I returned from rounding up stray cattle and I found out that Master Philemon had sent another servant to Colosse for supplies. By looking at me you could tell I was angry and I made a fool of myself!

Master Philemon was there when I returned to the big house "You look angry," he remarked. "What's wrong?"

"How can you ask that, Master?" I exploded. "I begged you to let me go to Colosse to get supplies so I could get more books, but while I was helping John, you sent someone else!"

"Onesimus!" This was the first time I had heard him raise his voice in this manner. I stared at him in surprised silence.

"It has been over a year since I sent a slave to the whipping post," he said with severe control. "I had hoped I would never have to again, but you are very near it now! If you get angry with me you'd better keep it from me." He paused and looked directly into my eyes. My silence prompted further query. "Did you hear me, Onesimus?"

"I hear you, Master," I replied in submission.

"You've every reason to be happy here," he continued. "Your work is light and privileges are many. Adjust or suffer the consequences. Is that understood?"

"Yes, Master."

He walked away.

Forget? No, I will never forget. I could not voice my anger and resentment, but it was there. I will never be happy here again, but I will learn to hate Master Philemon.

I settled into what appeared to be complete submission of my master's desires, occasionally treating some small illness or injury for one of the servants. Then one day there came the great test of my skills. Master Philemon's favorite mare broke her foreleg. She had fallen into a hole. John called another man and they kept her lying on her side until I could get there.

"Onesimus, do you think you can help her?" Philemon asked.

"I'll do my best, Master. Give me three men to help and a lot of strong rope. Also, I need several posts to place around her to tie her securely on her side. I'll set and bind the broken leg but she must lie on her side for three days. Then we'll turn her over very carefully so she can't put any weight on it."

"I know you'll do the best you can."

When the leg was set, we placed food and water within her reach. After staying with her for three weeks, turning her when necessary, I put her leg in a sling and drew it up toward her belly. She hobbled around a small enclosure on three legs for three more weeks. When the splint came off, we kept her tied to a post, allowing her to put her weight on her sore leg. After two more weeks of careful tending, it was evident she would be all right, and was ready to go back to the pasture.

Philemon examined her leg, and then hobbled her in her favorite patch of grass near the spring. Two weeks later, she was turned into the pasture with the other horses, as good as new.

"Thanks, Onesimus, you did a good job."

I looked at him in silence and gave a slight nod.

Another year had now passed since I found Martha only to lose her the same day. I wanted her more than anything in life, but she was out of reach. I quit reading and gave my attention to Pharaoh, riding him every day so he became attached to me, following me around like a favorite puppy. I rode him without a saddle except when Master Philemon sent me on an errand to one of the camps.

A pastor named Epaphras preached at Master Philemon's house once or twice a month. Sometimes he would stay a full month and do missionary work among the servants. The first day of the week was called the Lord's Day, and no work was done on that day except what was absolutely necessary. Though no servant was forced to attend the services, all were welcome. At times he would go into Colosse to teach. I didn't believe in this man that they called Jesus. I was raised to worship Diana, but I did not believe she was immortal. I believed in humanities, having been trained as a physician; therefore, I could not place Jesus, a mere man, above all other men.

One day I picked up a letter that a preacher named Paul had sent to Master Philemon. It was the first reading I had done in several weeks. Later I found the writings of Matthew and Luke. After that it was difficult for me to deny the resurrection of Jesus, yet I could not bring myself to accept it. I also noticed that all the Christians I met seemed happy and at peace, even servants who were believers. They demonstrated above average love and care for each other.

Me, I loved no one but Martha, whom I feared I might never see again, my mother and a horse that did not belong to me. I had become withdrawn and lost friends that I used to have. John, who had been a good friend, teaching me a lot about livestock, now seldom spoke because I was so full of resentment and anger.

One day John asked, "Onesimus, have I offended you? Why do you not speak to me?"

"I speak when spoken to," I retorted.

He gave me a strange look and stood there rubbing his hands on his garment, a habit he had when troubled.

"Well," he said slowly, "you've changed a great deal. You become angry for the smallest reason. You're not the cheerful person you were when you came. I'm sorry, Onesimus, but you're not pleasant to be around anymore."

"Have I become that bad, John?"

"Well," he replied, "You're uncivil most of the time and often rude. We'd all be happy for you to be your old self again."

I refused to listen to John or old Elias, who also tried to help me, but continued to wallow in bitterness. No one spoke to Philemon about me, and when he was around I obeyed him so he failed to note my hate and rancor.

One day Master Philemon came out where John and I were helping a cow with her first calf. He watched until the calf was standing. "That's a good job, a mighty good job," he said.

"Thanks, Master," John smiled, but I remained silent as though I didn't hear him.

"Onesimus, do you remember the way to the inn where you saved the gold for the innkeeper?" Master Philemon asked.

"Yes, Master."

"I'm buying the rest of his land in this area and I need you to take a payment to him. I'd go myself but I have to go to Ephesus on an important matter."

"I'll be glad to go for you, Master."

"You'll leave first thing in the morning. I'll have two bags of gold ready to deliver. You can ride Pharaoh and take plenty of provisions. Any questions?"

I thought for a moment then asked, "Will I be armed in case I need to defend myself and your gold?"

"Whatever you choose," he replied.

"I'd like to use the old Roman sword that I carried when we searched for the stolen horses," I requested.

"Very well," he replied as he walked away.

With very little sleep, I awoke just before sunrise to find that Elias had everything ready for me. Several weeks earlier, I had found an old mace and scraped all the rust off, keeping it in my room. I fastened it onto Pharaoh's saddle before I went to the big house.

I knew that this was my time to escape. I had to find Martha, and it was absolutely necessary to find my mother and deliver her from slavery. This was my chance. I was twenty-three years old and had never drawn a free breath, but now I'd have gold, I'd have Pharaoh, and weapons.

I was so obsessed with the prospect of becoming free that I lost all perspective of right and wrong. Reason eluded me, so I gave no thought to the fact that I would be a run-away slave with a price on my head, or that I would become a thief. All I could think of was freedom.

Just before Elias came to bid me farewell I had a tinge of remorse at leaving him, but thrust it from my mind. I justified all my wrong with the thought that I would become a great physician and help humanity.

I led Pharaoh to the steps where Elias waited.

"Do you remember what I told you the first time I met you?" he asked.

"You said, 'I once stood as tall as you do now. Time will come when you will stand as low as I do now.'"

"I'm glad it made an impression on you. Beware of pride and self-pity. They'll bring you more trouble than you can handle." He then firmly grasped my right hand and placed his other hand on my shoulder. As he looked me in the eye I felt he was reading my mind.

"Onesimus," he said, "if I could have had a son, I would have wanted him to be just like you. May God go with you."

Overcome with emotion, I could not reply. As I rode out of the yard I watched him walk up the steps. Tears burned my eyes as his last words rang in my head. "May God go with you."

I crushed my conscience into a tiny ball and relegated it to a remote crevice of my soul. "Elias knows I'm running away," I said aloud as Pharaoh's long legs ate up the miles.

I thought of the moral and ethical rules Mother taught me. "Oh, Mother," I cried, "what I'm doing is for the best because I can't be a slave any longer. Oh, Mother, please forgive me."

Suddenly I had a chilling thought. Master Philemon was not present when I rode away. Is he hidden along the trail to see if I take the gold to the innkeeper? My mind began to whirl.

Old Elias had thought of everything, even placing my sheepskin that I prized so highly over the two bags of gold. My sword and mace were within easy reach.

Pharaoh trotted for a while, and then I held him to a fast walk. I followed the trail that Philemon and I had first come over, but it seemed that many years had passed since then. I could not help wondering about Master Philemon. Perhaps he was ahead of me… or behind, watching me. Perhaps he guessed I might run away, but I felt certain Elias knew.

Needing to eat and allow the horse to rest, I walked a huge circle around my campsite to see if anyone was following. I saw nothing but a fox. After resting and eating a few bites, I rode on in the dark for an hour to evade the master, just in case he was following.

Crossing a little stream, I tied Pharaoh in some thick grass close to the water and prepared a small meal. I walked about two hundred yards into the thick brush and spread my sheepskin in a spot well hidden from anyone who might come to the campsite.

Before long I was dreaming that I was running away riding Hebel and Master Philemon, riding Pharaoh, was gaining on me. In desperation I tried to make Hebel go faster, but soon Philemon was upon me, waving his long sword and laughing at me. "You are mine," he yelled "I bought you with my own gold." Then he struck me with his sword.

I came wide-awake, shivering with fear, and with sweat standing on my face. It was still about three hours before sunrise, but I was soon in the saddle, riding away without eating. If Philemon was following, surely he could not find me now.

Pharaoh kept his fastest walk until noon. I climbed a little hill for a good view of the country behind me but I could see no one coming.

Late that evening I left the trail Philemon and I had come over and took a southwest direction. I remembered there was a good road running east and west beside the inn, and decided to intersect it several miles west of the inn.

Riding into rough country, I made slow progress after I left the trail. It was well after sundown before I found a spot fit for a campsite with grass and water for Pharaoh. After eating, I watched the stars come out and brighten the night with a soft glow, but I was afraid to go to sleep lest I should dream that awful dream again. I sat with my back against a tree and my sheepskin across my lap. I awoke sometime before daybreak so stiff and sore that I spread my sheepskin and went to sleep in a more comfortable position.

I awoke to the bright sun on my face and was glad for the extra sleep. This felt strange as I was accustomed to being up and dressed by sunrise. But I'm free now. Who cares if I sleep late? Suddenly my freedom took on a new dimension. I must now make all decisions for myself and I had never done that before. "It's all up to me, now," I said aloud. "Well, I'll do what I think is best, but right now I must decide whether to find mother or go to Rome. Which do you think will be best, Pharaoh?" I asked as I rubbed his smooth neck.

I finally decided to go to Rome and find Martha. Then, I reasoned, I'll go to Egypt, find Mother and bring her back to Rome where I'll establish myself as a physician.

After breakfast I allowed Pharaoh to find his way through the rough country as long as he was headed in the right direction.

I will use this gold to set up a house for us to live in and supply the office needs. Then, one day, when I begin to make a lot of money, I'll send repayment for this amount of gold back to Philemon. I'll also send enough to pay for Pharaoh and to repay him for the full amount he paid for me.

The decision to repay him as soon as I could, eased a very guilty conscience.

As there was no sign of a trail, it seemed I was riding where man had never ridden before. After three more grueling hours I came upon a small clearing. The trees had been cut many years ago and small ones had taken their place. Riding around the clearing, I found a mound of ashes, now overgrown with bushes. I reasoned that since a campfire never leaves such a big pile of ashes, it must have been a building. I found a little piece of the roof that had not burned. It had a vine growing through it. Who had lived in this lonely place? Why had he come here? Was he a runaway, too? Had he died here?

I hurriedly mounted and rode on through the wilderness. After an hour the terrain became more passable and I soon found a cattle trail going in my direction, so I followed it to a better trail.

Late that evening I saw a shepherd with his flock but I don't think he saw me. I did not want to be seen until I was far, far away from Philemon's home.

I camped that night in a safe place between two steep hills. I had a book Joash had given me and read until the fires died. Sleep came easily.

The next evening I came to a road running east and west and felt it was the one I sought. I guessed it must have been twenty miles or more back to the inn. I remembered the innkeeper had said there was not another inn on this road until the province of Caria. After traveling about ten more miles, I found the inn he mentioned.

A young lad came to care for Pharaoh.

"Feed him all he'll eat," I instructed.

"Yes, my lord," he replied "He's a big horse."

I took the two bags of gold and my camp outfit into the inn. My sword was attached to my girdle where it had been the last two days but I left the mace with the saddle.

Taking three pieces of gold from one of the sacks I fastened both sacks firmly inside my cloak, placed my camp outfit in one corner, and went to the dining room.

"Have you come far?" the innkeeper asked while I was eating.

"Very far," I replied.

When I paid for my meal and lodging the innkeeper said, "I get little gold here. Most travelers pay with silver."

"I've spent all my silver," I lied, "and I have only three gold pieces to last till I reach my destination."

"And where is that?" he asked.

I had already decided to say I was going to Amphipious in Macedonia, and that would throw no light on the fact that I was really going to Rome.

"Amphipious," I replied.

"How far is Miletus?" I asked breaking a long silence.

"I'm not sure. I've never been there but it's a good four day's ride from what I hear."

"Must be a hundred miles then," I suggested.

"Must be," he agreed "The road turns north about ten miles west of here. I've never been farther than that inn. From there I'm told the road turns west again and goes to Miletus."

After a fine meal and a glass of wine, I went to my room. Everything was as I had left it and soon I was asleep.

I awoke very early the next morning while everyone else was asleep, strapped on my sword and went to the corral. Pharaoh snorted softly as I walked into his stall. Soon we were headed west in the pre-dawn darkness.

As I had been told, I found the road turning north about ten miles from the inn. Riding on for two miles or more, I stopped and ate my breakfast. Not knowing how far we might have to go before finding water again, I gave Pharaoh ample time to nibble the lush grass and drink plenty of water.

Since it was late when I ate breakfast, I did not stop for a midday meal. In the middle of the afternoon I came to the inn that I had been told was the only one for many miles. I decided to stop for a hot meal and information about the road. I also needed to buy a few things to add to my provisions.

There were three men in the inn when I entered. As I sat at a long table to be served one of them got up and walked out. The steaming food was soon served and I realized I was hungrier than I thought.

In about ten minutes the crude-looking man returned. "That's a fine horse you have. Is he for sale?"

"Not at any price," I replied. "I'd rather lose an arm than lose him."

His rough looking companion was scraping something from his coat sleeve with a sharp dagger. He stared at me with malice and said, "You never lost an arm so how can you be sure?"

I ignored him and was making my purchase from the innkeeper when the questionable pair left the room. The third man, who had not spoken, walked over to me and said in a low voice, "You'd better watch those two. Either of them would kill you in a minute for that horse."

"Yes," the innkeeper added, shaking his head. "I don't like for them to stop at my place but they do from time to time."

I thanked them both for the warning and walked back to where Pharaoh waited for me. Riding several miles from the inn I found a suitable place to camp as it was growing dark. I discovered a pleasant, small waterfall tumbling off a rocky hill. It was an ideal spot with a good place to spread my sheepskin under the overhang of a large rock. It seemed so peaceful while I ate and studied. When I could no longer see to read, I stretched out under the rock.

As I slept, I dreamed my mother came to me. She looked as she did when young—so beautiful.

"What are you doing here, Mother?" I thought you were in Egypt."

She looked at me for some time then said in a sad voice, "My Son, I've come to warn you of great trouble ahead if you go through with this evil deed."

"But, Mother, I cried, "I'm a free man now, and what I'm doing is right."

"Don't do it, Son," she warned, then was gone.

I awoke to find myself standing, reaching out to her, but she was not there.

There were still a few coals where my fire had been so I threw dry leaves on them and soon had a blaze going again. I tried to read but could not concentrate. I fixed a small breakfast and rode out. A little past daybreak I met an old shepherd who told me of a much shorter way to Miletus.

"This road," he said, "goes too far south. It'll take you to Pedasus, and then roam around through the hills in a northwest direction to Miletus. It's crooked as a snake as it goes around the hills, but just over that first hill," he pointed with his staff, "you'll find a trail leading off to the right. Take that trail and keep on it. You'll find some more trails leading off to the right, but keep left. It's dim in places but if you travel by day you'll have no trouble staying on it."

"Are there any villages along the way?" I asked.

"No," he said stroking his beard. "No villages and no inns, but there are some shepherds along the way who have tents and would welcome your company for a night."

Since I wanted to be alone and save a few miles, I took the shortcut. I had plenty of provisions, so it didn't matter that there were no inns.

I rode through some lonely country. The trail kept rising gently until I must have been two thousand feet above the valley. I turned in my saddle and looked back. What a grand sight! I was on top of a small mountain and the whole world seemed to lie at my feet. As I looked back I saw two riders stop and talk to the old shepherd. From the motion of his hands he seemed to be telling them directions, and he pointed in my direction. The two riders took the trail at a fast trot.

"Well, now," I said aloud. "I wonder who they are. Are they trying to catch up with me? Maybe they know I'm carrying this gold, or maybe Philemon sent them after me and they've found my trail." I became worried as I remembered my mother's warning.

Whatever might be the answer, I didn't wait to find out. I went down the other side of the mountain at a fast run, and Pharaoh did run! I reached the bottom of the mountain a good while before they reached the top. They could not see me as the trail took a turn into some thick woods. There was a dry streambed filled with small rocks, so I left the trail and rode east about a mile. I unsaddled Pharaoh and staked him out on some rather thin grass. "It's the best I can do for you this time, old boy," I told him as I walked away.

I took my outfit and gold and walked back toward the trail for about two hundred yards, then turned north where I soon found a small hill thickly covered with trees. Not wanting them to see smoke, I sat with my back against a tree and ate a cold meal. Soon darkness closed in around me. I rolled in my sheepskin and went to sleep. I knew that they could not ride Pharaoh, even if they found him. He's a one-man horse and would throw anyone else, so I slept well.

It was still dark after breakfast when I walked back to Pharaoh, and I was soon on the trail headed for Miletus. I found tracks where the two riders had spent a little time. Searching for me and failing to find any vestige of Pharaoh's hoof prints, they obviously decided to go on. It made me angry to think I'd actually run from them.

"I'm a free man now," I told myself, "and I'll not run from them again. If they want me, they can have a taste of me and my sword."

I reasoned that they would ask another shepherd if I had been seen and would soon discover I was behind them. If so, I was sure they would come back to meet me or wait for me in ambush.

"Who are they?" I asked myself again. I doubt that they are from Philemon because I'm too far from his place now, but I did take his favorite horse and a goodly sum of his gold. I had not taken time to count just how much.

It must be the two men who wanted to buy Pharaoh back at the inn, I reasoned. Maybe they intend to steal him.

I began to ride with more caution, looking carefully before going around a bend and watching all the places where they might wait in ambush.

"Onesimus." Martha called. "The elder is here and he says it's urgent."

I laid my pen aside and painfully walked to the cave.

"Greetings, Brother Onesimus,"

"It's good of you to come," I replied.

"I'm glad to see you're still writing. How's it coming?"

"Well," I said, and then hesitated for a moment. "It's not half finished yet. I guess I'm still so weak that it is hard to work very long at a time."

"Ah, yes," he said. "You're very blessed to be here at all. Three more of our people have died from that beating. The Romans did it to please Caesar and to pacify some of the Jews who pay great sums to the army officers for their help."

Of course I knew the real reason for the stoning was because I'd been too outspoken against idolatry and the awful orgies that take place in service to idols. The Apostle Paul said it was a shame to even speak of those things they did in secret.

I remained silent, waiting for him to tell me the real reason he would walk twenty miles to see us. After several moments he said, "Brother Onesimus, the pagan priests and the oracle of Diana have sent spies to follow the saints who come here to see you. They now know where you are, and are determined to kill you at any cost. I think you should leave at once. Do you have another place to go?"

Jacobus spoke up, "Yes, I found another cave while hunting a week ago. It's about five miles to the south, well-hidden way up in the hills.

"Good, Jacobus. I suggest you take your family there immediately," the elder said. "I wish I could stay and help with the move, but I must hurry home. They're liable to strike my place at any time."

We bid the elder Godspeed as he left and immediately began preparations for another move.

Jacobus hitched the horse to the wagon, piled our few belongings in and helped me climb up. I took the reigns and drove a short distance. Jacobus took a leafy branch and swept the tracks away. He soon caught up, and taking the reigns, walked along beside the wagon.

It was almost dark before we reached the new cave so we camped in the entrance that night. The next day, everyone except me helped clean the new abode and place our belongings in it. By the second day we felt at home again. This was a fine cave to live in, very secluded and hidden from everyone.

"It's even better than the other one," Martha said cheerfully. The spring is nearer and the shade is better around the cave's mouth. No one could ask for a lovelier entrance than the one that that grand old tree provides."

"Yes," agreed Sarah. "I like it better because it's larger and gives more room to move about without bumping into each other." She laughed and patted her protruding belly.

That truly was a beautiful old tree that spread her huge branches a few feet from the cave, as if to protect it from intruders. It was early spring and the yellow-green leaves invited me to enjoy the sanctuary they furnished. I continued writing there when the weather allowed, and worked inside the cave at other times. Life in our new home, though rather lonesome at times, was very pleasant. The women spent a lot of time getting ready for the baby. Sarah's time was full and we had growing anticipation.

A few days later I was deep in thought with my book. The leaves rustling above my head blended with an occasional groan coming from the cave. Minutes later I heard the sharp squall of my first grandchild.

Elated, I stepped inside. The thrill of that moment was exceeded when Jacobus, bursting with pride, placed a squirming, tiny new form into my arms.

"You have a grandson, Papa."

I tried to swallow the lump in my throat as I remembered when Jacobus was born and said with a shaky voice, "I had forgotten a newborn baby is so small. What's his name?"

"We will call him Tychicus, named for our dear friend, Brother Tychicus."

That is a perfect name, I thought as I remembered that great Christian friend.

Chapter Seven

Ambushed

I rode on into the gathering dusk, looking for a good campsite. From the top of a little rise I saw a thick stand of trees with lots of grass. Turning from the trail, I decided to stay for the night. Leading Pharaoh and brushing out our trail, I backtracked for about a half mile before I found a rocky place to leave the trail. I then circled back through the woods to the spot I had previously chosen.

As my life might depend on it, I was learning to leave no trail. These were evil days and human life was cheap, especially to those who lived by killing and taking what they wanted.

After staking Pharaoh in the best grass, I made a cold camp. I felt sure the two men had not given up, and I didn't want them to smell smoke. It grew cold after dark so I rolled up in my sheepskin and lay there looking at the stars, only a few at first, then the sky was full of them. I wondered how Mother was faring, but soon Martha's sweet face came before me. I wondered if she was enjoying living in Rome with her Uncle Abraham.

I will find her, I told myself drifting to sleep, my sword and dagger within easy reach.

By the time there was enough light to make a pale shadow, I was again headed toward Miletus. The trail became so rocky that I sometimes had trouble deciding which way it turned. When I passed the rocky ground a beautiful valley lay before me. Soon I saw a shepherd watching as his sheep grazed near a little stream and decided to question him.

"Good morning," I called. "Have you seen two men ride past within the last few hours?"

"Yes," he scratched his head and carefully looked me over before continuing. "Two rode by yesterday about two hours before dark."

"Did they speak with you?"

"No, but they did speak with Ham. I don't think they saw me. I was way up this stream at that time."

"Where may I find Ham?"

"His flock is just around the next hill. He thinks the grass is better there," he replied with a grin.

"Thanks, and have a pleasant day," I said as I waved.

"Ham is my brother and he's also a great talker. He'll talk to you half the night," he said as I rode away.

If they rode past here two hours before dark yesterday, I reasoned, they're still a few hours ahead of me. Since I don't want to catch them, I won't travel too fast; however, if I do meet them again, I refuse to run. If they decide I'm still behind them, they'll probably ambush me somewhere along the trail, or they might ride back to meet me. One thing is sure, I'll ride with extreme caution.

I located Ham beside a small spring. Its water flowed between two hills and then formed a beautiful little lake.

After a polite greeting, I asked, "Did you see two men ride by here about two hours before dark yesterday?"

"Yes." I waited for him to continue but he was silent.

"Did they ask any questions?" I persisted.

"They wanted to know if you had ridden by before they got here."

"How can you tell they were asking about me? You've never seen me before."

"No, I don't know you," he answered, "but they said you were very tall with rather wide shoulders and were riding the most wonderful horse they had ever seen. So, when you rode up I said to myself, *now that's the person those two were asking about yesterday*."

I dismounted and led Pharaoh to water. Ham came over and placed his hand on Pharaoh's neck.

"Did they say or ask anything more about me?" I continued.

"One of them said that if you should ask about them, that I should say they only asked about the road ahead."

"And why are you telling me the truth?"

"Because, I never promised to tell a lie for them. I've always tried to be truthful, and beside that, I didn't like their looks," he said with emphasis. As he patted Pharaoh's forehead he continued, "This is indeed a beautiful horse."

"The best I've ever seen, I replied."

"They told me that you were carrying gold," he said."They went outside the inn where you were buying supplies. Through a crack in the wall, they saw you take gold from a bag."

I listened silently.

"One of them said he saw you a few years back with a man named Philemon, and that you stampeded his horses and killed some of his men. He means to kill you and take your horse," Ham said.

Not knowing what to say, I remained silent. I wondered if they told him I was a runaway, or did they know that?

Ham was a friendly man and had already told me enough to let me know he wasn't a partner with the thieves. I decided to tell him the truth as I was badly in need of a friend right now.

"I believe you're being truthful with me," I said, "so I'll be truthful with you. I'm a runaway. My size, my youth, and this great red horse are facts I cannot change. I do have a bag of gold. I took it…I was to deliver it to a man whom my master owed, but I took it and ran away." I was beginning to feel much better. I could look him in the eye and let him know I'm a man, even if I am a runaway slave.

Ham walked away to send the dog after a stray sheep. I unsaddled and staked the horse. Ham seemed to be well educated, and that is unusual out here in this lonely country. While I was putting the finishing touches on my meal, Ham came up to my fire.

"I was a slave for three years," he said. "I was taken by a band of thieves and sold to a Roman officer. My brother learned where I was and helped me escape. We came to this country, where there is little chance of being found, and started raising sheep. You need not fear either of us."

"Thank you," I said sincerely. "It's good to find a friend." He seemed deep in thought so I continued, "I was born a slave and have never been free until now."

"Until many years have gone by or all that know you are dead, you'll never be really free," he said. Many people would kill you for that horse."

"You don't speak as an average man," I said. "You sound as though you read a lot."

"Yes, I read in three languages."

"That's interesting." I was surprised.

"I've read some of the writings of Pythagoras and some works of Aristophanes, especially his comedies. I've attempted to read some of Aristotle's books, but I get lost in his technical philosophies."

"Well," I said, "I'm surprised to see an educated man in this wilderness tending sheep."

He smiled. "I was a teacher in one of the best schools until an enemy managed to have me sold. I live here in seclusion now, but there is a serene peace out here that I never experienced when I was among mankind.

"I met a girl and I intend to find her," I told him. "She's possibly living in Rome with her uncle. I'll be unnoticed among the multitude."

We were both silent for several moments, then talked for a couple of hours about books and philosophers.

Feeling I had found a new friend, I told my life story.

"I haven't seen my mother since Master Philemon bought me, so..." my mind trailed.

It's been a long time since I've been able to talk to an educated man," Ham said.

"Well, it's certainly a delight to talk with you," I assured him. "I would like to stay several days, but I must be on my way."

"You're welcome to stay as long as you will," Ham said.

"I really can't stay. I expect trouble from those two thugs, so I'd better get moving."

"You may sleep here tonight," Ham said. "No one can come near my camp without my knowledge. Those are two great watchdogs."

"Thank you. I'll be glad to share your camp tonight but I'll leave by first light."

"I wish you success in finding your girl in Rome," he said with a friendly smile.

In a short time Ham was asleep. I made plans for the future, and then slept comfortably.

Early the next morning we ate a hot meal and I was soon on my way. I felt as though I was leaving a brother.

"May the gods go with you," he called after me.

When I reached the top of the hill, about a quarter of a mile from camp, I turned in the saddle and waved. "And may the gods guard you, my friend," I said under my breath.

Watching the tracks of two riders slowed me and I didn't make very good time that day. Just before dark the tracks disappeared, so I rode back a ways and found where they had left the trail. I supposed they were camping near by. That night I went to sleep almost as soon as I drew my sheepskin around me and slept about an hour later than usual.

The next morning their trail was plain. Realizing they were now ahead of me again, I reasoned that I must confront these two as soon as possible, otherwise I could not rest or ride safely.

About noon I asked a herdsman how long since they had seen two men ride by.

He looked me over as though he wasn't going to answer, then said, "I want no trouble," and walked away. I figured they had threatened him and were probably close by watching.

Continuing on the trail, I felt a little nervous tinge run up my back. I loosened my sword and dagger, then untied my mace and hung it on the saddle with a loose loop. Touching my heel to Pharaoh's flank I rode swiftly down the trail. Refusing to run from them again, I decided that if they wanted a fight, I would give it to them.

About a mile down the trail they had selected a spot where I couldn't go around them. On my right was a small hill going almost straight up for about ten feet, and on my left was dense, impassable undergrowth and trees. They had separated themselves by the narrow trail, so I would have to turn and run or go between them. About thirty yards from them I drew my sword with my right hand and held the mace in my left. I kicked Pharaoh rather hard and he sprang into a fast run. I gave a savage yell and kicked him again.

Pharaoh's and my great size, my savage yell, and our flashing speed were too much for them. Being totally unprepared for such actions, they sat in their saddles. Their selection of a place to meet was in my favor since they could not escape. Wide-eyed with astonishment, they managed to draw swords just as I was upon them. As Pharaoh dashed between them, I struck the man on the left with my mace, jerking him from his mount. The man on my right swung to the other side of his horse and my sword passed harmlessly above his head. He ran down the trail leaving his friend.

Quickly I returned to the fallen man, dismounted and tied Pharaoh to a tree. The mace had caught him in the neck leaving a terrible gash. The great vein had been severed and blood spurted with each heartbeat. He looked at me with terror in his eyes.

"Don't be afraid of me," I said. "I'm a physician and it's not my nature to kill. I'm sorry it happened like this."

He tried to speak but only blood came from his mouth. There was nothing I could do but kneel on the trail beside him and sadly watch him die.

After mounting Pharaoh, I rode slowly with a terrible feeling of guilt. If I had not run away, this never would have happened. I have been trained to save lives, now I had taken one. The gold I was carrying suddenly lost its value when I compared it to the human life I'd just taken. Having no means of burying the thief, I continued on the trail.

Coming to a little stream, I stopped to let Pharaoh drink. I washed the blood from my mace and myself, but I knew that water could never wash away my guilt.

Late that evening I made camp but had trouble sleeping. I tried to think of mother or Martha, but that dying man's terror-filled eyes haunted me.

Late the next day I rode into Miletus, located on the south side of the Meander River where it runs into the Aegean Sea, about thirty-five miles south of Ephesus.

Finding a nice inn, I remained there for three days. I rode over the town, giving everyone a chance to see me. If I was wanted there, I would soon know, but no one seemed to take note of me, although several took a second look at Pharaoh. I finally decided that no one knew I was a run-away slave.

According to what Martha had told me, her relatives were going to live in Ephesus, so I decided to go there, and then take a boat to Rome. I paid my account at the inn and rode out.

It should have taken me only one day to ride to Ephesus, but I took my time and enjoyed the countryside. I reached the outskirts of the city just before dark the next day. Planning to stay about a week, I took a room.

I inquired diligently about Martha's family who had come approximately two and a half years before, even saying the small lad had broken his arm and would still have had it in a sling, but no one could remember them.

I enjoyed talking with Plautus, the innkeeper. He had done everything possible to make my stay comfortable. One day I described Martha in the best detail I could, but all my prompting failed to bring her to his mind.

"Well," I remarked, "I'll go on to Rome and search there."

"You have an odd name," Plautus said. "I've never heard it before."

I've heard yours before," I smiled. "I've read some of the writings of the great Roman Plautus who translated Greek drama into Latin. He also wrote some comedy in Latin."

"Never heard of him," he replied. "I've never learned to write much more than my name, but I can read a little Hebrew. My mother was a Jew and she taught me what little she knew."

By the end of the week we had become fast friends and I felt I could trust Pharaoh into his care. I decided I liked Ephesus so much that I would find Martha and return to set up my practice there.

Knowing Pharaoh's loyalty to me, I had several times taken him out to ride and held him for Plautus to mount. He was beginning to trust Plautus who promised to feed him well and to exercise him a couple of times a week until I returned from Rome. I paid him in advance and told him that if I failed to return within six months, I would repay him when I did return.

I packed most of my things, including the mace, and left them in storage with Plautus. I wore my sword and kept the dagger hidden in my girdle. Being fond of my sheepskin, I kept it with me.

"When I return," I said, "I plan to establish myself here in Ephesus as a physician."

"That's good news," he said. "We have one doctor here now, but he is not able to get around as he once did."

"There are men who will steal my horse if they can. Please watch him carefully."

"Don't worry, Onesimus," he said. "I'll see that he is here and in good shape. Have a good trip and hurry back."

The next day I boarded a ship for Rome. I loved the sea and we had a good trip except for one night. A storm hit suddenly while the ship was under full sail. The ship almost overturned before the Captain could get the sails down and head her into the waves. The storm passed over in about three hours and once more we were headed for Rome.

We landed first at Ostia, where repairs were made to the ship and sails before we proceeded up the Tiber River. What a grand sight to see Rome, the most powerful city on earth, with its captains and centurions drilling their troops daily. Mounted soldiers paraded through the great city with standards waving. A carnival spirit was everywhere.

I left the ship and sought an inn far from the waterfront, as I knew it to be a stronghold for robbers, murderers, and women who were as bad as, if not worse than the men. After walking the streets for about five hours, I found a place I felt would be safe. Polybius, the proprietor, told me that he was named for a Greek statesman who wrote much about Rome.

"I've never read any of his work," I said.

"Well," he said, "he had his start in Greece where he became an officer and fought in the wars for Rome, but he was accused of being an enemy of Rome and was sent here for a military trial. He won the friendship of several powerful senators who helped him win his trial. He and his family stayed here, so he did much to help the Greeks escape the wrath of Rome."

"That's interesting," I replied "I'd like to read some of his writings someday."

Polybius stepped down from a high stool on which he had been sitting, and motioned for me to follow. He led me to a room where there were two large shelves full of scrolls. "Help yourself to as many as you want to read. Just be sure to place them back in order when you're finished with them.

"Oh," I exclaimed with gratefulness, "I love to read."

Selecting two different authors, I took them to my room and read until midnight.

The next morning I set out to make a few friends. When speaking to the Romans, I was careful to use their language, so they never seemed to doubt that I was one of them. There were few Jews in this part of the city, and when I found one, I always asked about Martha and Uncle Abraham, who was a tentmaker, but no one knew them.

The inn where I was staying was about eight streets south of the Palantine Hill where the Imperial Palace was located, and a little southeast of the Aventine Hill, just off the Ostian Road. I rented a horse and continued my search. I learned that there was an amphitheater on the extreme east side of Rome, so I went there to get acquainted with some of the military. They often rode with caravans to protect them, and it might be that one of them rode with the one that brought Martha to Rome. It was a slim chance, but I intended to do everything possible to find her. She had said, "I'll wait at Uncle Abraham's place in Rome." How I wish she could have told me just where it was located.

The road to the Amphitheater lay along the southern edge of the Caelian Hill. I enjoyed the ride since there were many homes, real palaces, along the way. Children played around most of the houses where flowers and fruit trees grew in profusion. I was riding between the southern wall of the city and the Caelian Hill. The further I rode, the more soldiers I saw. I talked with them frankly and told them I was looking for a Hebrew girl named Martha and her Uncle Abraham. Most of them were civil, but a few were brusque, glaring at me when I mentioned a Hebrew name. Finally

I met a soldier who told me I was looking in the wrong part of Rome if I wished to find a Hebrew.

"Why?" I asked.

"There is a large area on the other side of the Tiber River and most people you will find there will be Jewish," he explained.

"Thank you, Sir. Will you direct me to the Jewish quarter?"

"Go back the way you came until you get to the Latin Road, then go west until you reach the northern slope of Aventine Hill. You'll then come to the Trigemine Gate. Go through that gate and on to cross the Tiber River on the bridge of Probus. You'll find yourself in the Jewish area."

I thanked him and rode toward the Tiber River.

In the Jewish quarter I was very careful to speak Hebrew. I first looked for a room to use while searching for Martha, and found a nice inn situated near the heart of the settlement. It was a clean place just south of the Aurelian Road that ran through the Jewish colony. My room was larger than the one at Polybius' place.

I discovered the Jews to be more tranquil than the Romans. They were quieter and the spirit of revelry and entertainment were not so rife among them. The innkeeper's name was Haggai and I liked him at once. I hated to leave Polybius' but felt it was necessary to my mission so I moved my things to Haggai's place.

My command of Hebrew caused them to accept me. Having studied the books of Moses and most of the writings of David and Daniel, I was able to take part in their religious conversation. I seemed right at home and liked it.

Soon I learned about the organization of Zealots. They were opposed to Rome and the Jews who tried to live peaceably with the Romans. There was a tension between the two factions of Jews who imposed an uncomfortable feeling on many occasions. The Zealots tried to stay underground to do their secret work, but their fanaticism often surfaced and they were detected. They were a clandestine order, and I overheard some talk one night that no one was supposed to hear. The next day I mentioned the Zealots to my host. He registered surprise and fear.

"We never discuss the Zealots in my inn," Haggai said. "We live among the Romans and they allow us to worship Jehovah according to our law. We have our synagogues and the Romans leave us alone. We want to keep it like that."

"I assure you," I replied, that I merely want information. I know there are some of them about, and I felt I should know their intentions. Rest assured that I share your attitude toward the Romans."

"Thank you," he replied gravely. "I'm so happy that you're a reasonable man."

Just then the man I overheard talking about the Zealots walked in. Haggai turned away and began to arrange a shelf of scrolls that seemed to be in perfect order. I kept the man in my peripheral vision so I could detect it if he moved a finger. After he sat down, I casually moved to another table to keep him in better view

Haggai tried to pretend he did not see the man who, after a few minutes called loudly, "Is it possible to get service in this god-forsaken place?"

"Jehu," Haggai began, "You know I don't want your trade and I don't want you in my inn. You are a threat to all I hold dear. Please go and stay away from here." He spoke in a low voice but his words carried a weight that I could feel as well as hear.

The Zealot turned and looked at me I still carried my sword so it was at my side. My dagger was also in plain view. Since most men carried arms, mine attracted no undue attention. Jehu stood facing Haggai. "I'll see you again when your bodyguard isn't with you. It'll be different then, I assure you." He stormed out of the inn.

When we were alone, Haggai said, "I'm glad you were here. Jehu is a dangerous man. Most Zealots are bad, but he is one of the worst. It's common knowledge that he has already killed three men, though no one will testify against him for fear of retaliation. I hate the name, Zealot!"

"I believe he could stick a dagger in your back if he were to meet you on a dark street," I noted.

"You may have noticed that I never go out at night. Many of our people have been cast out of Rome because of the actions of a few Zealots. They aren't doing their dirty work for the Jews, but they have some illicit aim in mind." Haggai rubbed his hand across his balding head in deep thought. "I don't understand their motives."

I questioned, "Have you decided the best policy for now is to say nothing?"

"That's right," he answered.

We never mentioned the Zealots again.

I made friends around the inn. Some were powerful men, respected by Jews and Romans, but Haggai became my best friend.

After breakfast one morning I put some coins in my money belt—a few more than usual—and put the others in my camp outfit and covered it with my sheepskin before going on my daily search. It seemed that Martha was a favorite name among the Jews, and I also found three men named Abraham, but none was a tentmaker.

That evening, as I trudged along the Aurelian Road on the way back to the inn, I met a stranger and asked him about Martha.

"Yes, my Lord," he said "I believe I can help you."

Hope sprang in my heart. At last I had a clue. "Thank you," I said.

"I can't tell you because I don't know the names of the streets, but if you will give me a small coin, I'll take you there."

"I'll give you a silver coin now and another when I find the right Martha," I promised.

"It's a very long way from here," he said as he received his coin. "She lives on the other side of the settlement, down by the river."

He started down the street with me at his heels. It was already about half an hour before sundown. I remembered that Haggai told me that many Zealots lived by the river, so I had not searched that area. As I followed my guide through the waning day, I felt sure I would not find her in this evil place. The further we walked the more noise and bawdiness we heard. There were painted women plying their wicked trade along the streets. Some, already too drunk to walk, just leaned against a wall or sat on the ground.

"I don't believe Martha would live in this filth," I stopped and said. "She's a good woman and could never endure this for one day."

"Yes, yes," he agreed, "she's a fine woman. It's just a little further to her house."

I wanted to turn back. It had grown dark so I loosened my sword and placed my hand on my dagger. Something seemed very wrong, but I couldn't afford to turn down my first clue.

We were near the river where all kinds of unholy characters stayed indoors all day and came out at night to do mischief. I heard gruff laughter and high-pitched voices as drunken men and women reveled in orgies and riotous merry-making. Fear flooded over me and I wanted to flee—to run back to the inn where there would be quiet, intelligent conversation.

"There's her house." The guide pointed to a shack standing near the riverbank. "Ah, the door's open." He walked into the dark room calling her. "Come on in," he invited. "She'll be here in a minute."

Something felt very wrong, but I stepped just inside, squinting to see in the darkness. Suddenly a heavy object fell on my head and I went to the floor. I seemed to see thousands of stars, and then total darkness.

"I'm tired, Martha," I said as I cleaned some drying ink from my pen.

I have been obsessively working to complete my life's story, but my internal injuries are not healing. *There can't possibly be much time left to write,* I thought, as we walked hand in hand to the cave, but I have to rest for a while.

A soft drizzle had begun falling, and gave a good reason to go in. "Jacobus," called Martha, "help your papa into his chair."

I sat for a moment drinking in the beauty of our newest cave-home. Jacobus and the women had done wonders to make it comfortable.

Only one elder, who comes about once a month, knows where we live, and he's careful not to be followed.

We have plenty of fish and game in these hills, and Jacobus uses his great skill to keep us well supplied. Once every five or six weeks, he puts on a disguise and goes into Gubbio to see how the other Christians are managing, and to bring back fresh supplies.

Jacobus is an excellent hunter so we have plenty of fresh meat and fish most of the time. Using a disguise, he goes into town once every six weeks to see how other Christians are doing and to bring fresh supplies.

I looked at Martha who was reading a page of my story. She glanced at me with her incredible smile and began to read, "*Hypnotized by her eyes, I sat there numb, speechless…she smiled and my heart began to pound.* My precious Onesimus," she teased, "did I really have that effect on you?"

She cuddled close beside me and I kissed her soft lips.

"My beautiful Martha," I whispered trying not to awaken little Tychicus. "You had that effect then, and even more so now. You truly are a gift from God."

I've had a wonderful day with my family, resting and playing with Tychicus. He's growing very fast and I cherish every moment I have with him. I wish I could hold him and play with him, but my pain is growing worse every day, and I fear I will not finish this book. I will write a little more today, with God's help.

How long have I been lying face down in a pool of blood? Was it one day? Maybe two or three, I wondered but had no way of knowing.

I looked carefully around the filthy room before I tried to get up. Sunshine streamed in the open doorway, bringing with it the stench from the river and garbage that lined the streets. I heard no sound except the distant call of a bird. A lean, brown dog walked slowly across the street, came to the door and looked at me in silence, wagging his tail and quizzically turning his head from side to side. He came when I called him, and sniffed my face, but he slowly walked away. I tried to stand, but sank back in pain onto the bloody floor. In the distance I heard a baby crying.

Looking around the dingy room, I wondered if I belonged here. I felt a gash in the top of my head and vaguely remembered being struck. Perhaps I should get up and go someplace, but where? I forced myself to my feet and walked about three steps to the door. Cold sweat shrouded my body and my ears began to ring. The sounds of singing birds and the crying baby faded as the bright light quickly paled to blackness and I buckled to a heap in the open doorway.

Gradually I came to my senses as if someone were pulling a dark cloth from my eyes. I heard distant voices that slowly became clearer, and I began to understand what they were saying.

"Where did you find him?" a voice asked.

"He was in an old deserted house down by the river. I had gone to take some food and clothing to a poor woman and her child. He evidently tried to walk but fell and struck his head on a rock just outside the door. That bruise on his forehead is probably from that fall, but that awful gash on top of his head was put there earlier by someone else, I'm sure of that. I saw a large pool of dried blood inside the room."

"Things like this happen all the time down on the riverfront," another voice added.

"Let me look at him." This voice seemed familiar to me. I tried to see him but my vision was blurred.

"Say, I know him," the voice said. "That's Onesimus, Brother Philemon's slave."

"Are you sure, Epaphras?"

"Yes, I'm sure, Brother Paul. I've seen him many times when I preached at Philemon's."

"When did you last see him?" Paul questioned.

"The last time I visited Philemon. You remember, Brother Paul, I was arrested and put in jail here with you right after I left there the last time," Epaphras replied.

My mind was clearing and I opened my eyes. This was not the room where I was attacked. I remembered why I had gone there, and realized I had been knocked out and robbed. I felt for my money belt but it was missing. My sword and dagger were also gone.

"How do you feel, Onesimus?" Epaphras asked.

"I must be some better," I replied in Latin. "At least I can see. Who brought me here?"

"Luke and Tychicus," the Apostle Paul said.

They gave me a bowl of warm soup that I gulped down as darkness began to invade the room.

Someone lit two candles that threw distorted shadows across the walls. Paul was in chains, but this was obviously not a prison. Later I learned that he was allowed to live in a house that he himself had rented. Sometimes he was chained to a Roman soldier, other times to a great stone placed at the side of the house. The chain was long enough for him to move freely from his bed to the table, to his desk and to the scroll shelves. I had heard much about the great Apostle Paul. He was highly educated and respected.

Before they went to sleep, Luke read from a large scroll. They sang songs to their God, songs with smooth sounds and soothing words.

Between a severe pain in my head and two men snoring, I could hardly sleep. That night I lay thinking about how Mother had warned me in a dream that if I continued with my plan to run away, I would suffer.

"Oh, Mother," I cried quietly, "You were so right. These men will surely send me back to Philemon in chains. I'll never be able to find you or Martha. Please come to me again and tell me what to do." Hot tears streamed down my face. *I'll never be a physician now*, I thought. *Philemon will sell me and I'll probably spend the rest of my life serving some cruel master."*

Finally I slept, edgily.

Chapter Eight

Living with the Disciples

With a breakfast call I stood dizzily on wobbly legs and Tychicus directed me to a large wash-basin just outside the door. The cold water was soothing to my feverish face and hands. My throbbing wounds had been dressed with olive oil.

After breakfast I glanced around the very large room as I listened to Paul and Luke discussing religious doctrine, while Epaphrus and Tychicus silently cleaned the dishes. As Tychicus swept the floor, I noticed there was plenty of space for several sleeping mats to be spread. There were doors on the north and south sides, and a large window on the east where a table stood, filled with scrolls, ink pot and quills. In the center of the room was another long table with benches, which would amply serve at least eight or ten people. A large fireplace surrounded with cooking utensils occupied the west wall.

This was a strange group. Though they were serious and seldom said anything that caused laughter, they smiled a lot. I had met Epaphrus several times at Philemon's home, and had seen Tychicus once. I later learned that Epaphrus was arrested for refusing to bow to the Roman emblem that the soldiers carried, but since this was not a serious offense, he was not in chains. Paul was in chains as a political prisoner as well as a Christian rebel.

Epaphrus hung up a dishcloth and sat across the table from me.

"Well, Onesimus, you look like you might be able to talk now. Did Philemon send you to Rome on a business errand?"

I thought I could say I was on an errand and they might let me go so I could find Martha, but about that time Paul sat beside Epaphrus, his heavy chains scraping across the wooden bench. I looked into his piercing eyes and knew he would detect a lie.

"I ran away from Master Philemon," I mumbled, looking down at the table.

"Do you want to tell us about it?" asked Tychicus as he sat beside me.

Why did the Apostle Paul not speak? His silent gaze terrorized me. Did he hold me in contempt? I'd heard Philemon say that Paul was the most wonderful person he'd ever met. Master Philemon had told me that Paul had performed several miracles there in Philemon's house. He and several others had traveled all the way to Laodicia to hear the great Apostle preach when he went there to organize a church. Why did he not speak to me now?

"If you don't want to talk now we'll wait until you feel better," Epaphrus said.

I realized I had been so lost in thought that I had not replied. "Thank you. I'd rather tell you about it later."

During the day, they went about their duties but no one spoke to me. I felt embarrassed and out of place. I knew one sect in Egypt that punished their children by refusing to speak to them.

They prayed together and sang several hymns and Psalms throughout the day, and spent much time reading silently. I wanted to read but my eyes were out of focus. I knew it would be weeks before I could read again and might even have poor eyesight the rest of my life.

Luke came in just after dark and sat at the table. The Apostle Paul looked at him for a moment then said, "I see you have bad news."

"Another brother has been tortured until he recanted," Luke replied sadly.

"Did you know him?" Paul questioned.

"I've met him a time or two. His name is Malchi. He endured a terrible beating, but when they brought the fire, he gave up and denied the Lord Jesus," Luke explained.

"How sad," Paul expressed. "We must pray much for the power of the Gospel to move among the workers of iniquity and turn them to Jesus Christ. We Christians must make up our minds to be faithful unto death, as our Lord commands."

"Yes," replied Luke. "Hundreds are dying daily here in Rome and in Jerusalem where the Jews are persecuting them."

"What happened after Malchi recanted?" asked Paul.

"They left him tied to the stake, bleeding to death from the beating they had given him. When the soldiers left, I stopped the bleeding and took him to another brother's home. I trust he'll recover and return to the Savior."

"I pray he will," Paul said sadly.

"The Zealots are doing all they can to stir up the Romans against the Christian Jews," Epaphrus said. "Is this Malchi a Jew?"

Luke nodded.

"Not only that," added Epaphrus, "they also enflame the Jews against the Romans."

"It's no wonder they're called dagger-men," Luke said. "Several have been stabbed lately, and some have died in the Jewish settlement. Many think the Zealots are doing the dirty work."

"But no one is brave enough to testify against them in court, even if they witnessed it," Epaphrus said.

"We must not become bitter against all Zealots," Paul exhorted. "Just remember that our Lord Jesus selected a Zealot as one of his twelve apostles."

Everyone sat in silent thought, as Paul continued, "Even the Zealots make good Christians when the Lord saves them from their sins."

They continued to eat in silence, then there came a hurried knock on the door and a man called for Luke.

"What do you want with him?" asked Paul.

"A soldier struck a man with his mace when he didn't move out of his way fast enough, and he's in terrible pain," he gasped, seeming to be tired from running. "He needs a physician."

"I do hope," said Luke, grabbing his bag, "there's not a broken bone. I'm trained in medicine but know little about bones."

"I've set many broken bones," I said as I stood.

"Then, if you feel able, come with me," Luke invited. "I didn't know you were a physician."

"I had forgotten about it," Epaphrus said, "but Philemon said Onesimus was a good doctor."

"Please bring some wood for splints, some winding cloth, and olive oil," I requested.

Although I was not steady on my feet, we hurried for about a mile and found the groaning man under a tree. Not only was his arm broken, but also his hip was badly bruised by a second blow.

By the time we were ready to work on his arm, Epaphrus caught up to us with the things I had requested. Soon the arm was splinted and the old man was more at ease.

I treated the bruised hip and, with the help of a stick that Luke handed him, he was able to walk. I refused the few small coins he graciously offered.

Feeling light-headed from my injuries, I found a large rock and sat down until I could regain some strength. I felt dreadful but believed I would be all right.

"Onesimus," Luke said, "I had no idea you were trained in medicine."

I smiled then said, "Master Luke, are you the one who dressed my wounds?"

"Yes, Onesimus, and I know you feel terrible but you are young and healthy and should heal very quickly."

As Epaphrus, Luke and I leisurely walked back to Paul's prison house in the cool night air, we discussed my medical training and goals.

As we entered, Paul and Tychicus were studying a scroll.

"Brother Paul," Luke said, "Onesimus did an excellent job on that arm and hip."

"Ah," he smiled, lifting one eyebrow and slightly tilting his head in pleasant surprise. I had already been around him long enough to recognize this as one of his mannerisms. "So we have two physicians—Luke and Onesimus,".

It seemed the fresh night air had cooled my fever, and though my headache was worse, I suddenly realized I no longer had double vision.

I went to bed a distressed man that night. These men spoke of Jesus Christ as though he was alive in a resurrected body, and he was actually sitting in heaven on the right hand of their God. I had heard that gods live in heaven, but I found it hard to believe that a man could be crucified then rise from the dead and ascend into heaven on a cloud.

After tiring of trying to understand about this man Jesus, I turned my thoughts to Martha. *What if she's forgotten me? We only met that one time. Maybe she met another man or even worse, what if she's married?* My fears were overcome again when I heard her sweet voice say, "I'll wait for you at Uncle Abraham's place in Rome." I held to that promise.

In my troubled sleep, I dreamed that Martha was riding Pharaoh, her long black hair streaming in waves behind her as she tried to escape my touch. I called for him to stop but he only ran faster and faster, causing a terrified Martha to scream for help while holding on for life.

"Wake up, Onesimus," Epaphrus called and shook me "You're yelling in your sleep."

I sat up and looked around. They were all staring at me.

"Did you have a bad dream?" asked Epaphrus.

"I certainly did," I answered, running my hand across my sore head. I was still shaking and cold sweat stood in beads on my bruised brow. It was a long time before I managed to sleep again.

The next morning I arose with Epaphrus and helped with breakfast.

"You cook?" he questioned.

"Since I was six or seven," I answered.

"Well," Paul spoke from his mat, "we have a slave who is a physician, a cook, and speaks Latin and Hebrew."

"I also speak Arabic and Greek," I said matter-of-factly.

"Well," Paul exclaimed, "How did you manage all that as a slave?"

After explaining, I said lowering my eyes, "And…" I tightened my jaw and in anger spoke through my clenched teeth. "Now here I am, a run-away."

Paul watched me a long time before speaking. "Do you still like to read?"

"Yes, Master," I answered submissively, having gained some control of my emotions.

After breakfast Luke read from the book of Isaiah and they all prayed before starting their chores.

"Onesimus," the Apostle Paul said, "would you like to read my letter to the Ephesian saints?"

"Certainly," I assured him as I began pouring over the lines. It was different from anything I had ever read. It seemed to be saturated in a mysterious doctrine I had never heard before. I came to the place where Paul wrote,

> *Which he wrought in Christ, when he raised him from the dead, and sat him at his own right hand in heavenly places, far above all principality, and power, and might, and dominion, and every name that is named, not only in this world, but also in that which is to come: and hath put all*

> *things under his feet, and gave him to be head over all things to the church, which is his body, the fullness of him that filleth all in all.*

I went back and read that passage again, then sat, looking out the window thinking about what I'd read. How did Paul know God raised Jesus from the dead? What evidence was there to prove that Jesus was alive, sitting at the right hand of God? How could Paul prove that Jesus was above all powers both in heaven and in earth? Was he greater than Diana, and Apollo, and Zeus, or, even Moses?

I put the scroll back on the shelf. My head was beginning to hurt worse and my vision blurred. I walked out into the fresh air and sunshine where I could understand natural things. I could not understand how a human could come back from the dead and have power over all others. I sat under a tree and meditated for a long time. *Interesting, but I don't understand,* I thought, literally shaking my head in order to try to clear my mind.

What I do understand is that I have to decide how to find Martha. If they don't send me back to Philemon, I told myself, *I'll go to Ephesus and establish my practice. The next time someone offers me a few coins for my services, I'll accept, since all my gold was stolen.*

Epaphrus called, so I went inside.

"You promised to tell us why you left Philemon," he stated bluntly.

I knew Epaphrus was a disciple, who was well thought of in Colosse and had established a church in Philemon's house, but I resented his questioning me, so I sat tacitly, looking with defiance toward the wall.

"Onesimus." The Apostle Paul's tone let me know he was in authority as he finally broke the silence. "Philemon is a special friend of mine. He's my son in the Gospel of Jesus Christ because I won him to the Lord from the world of idolatry. If you've wronged him, I demand that you tell me about it."

"There are several sides to my running away, Master. It will require a lot of time to tell the whole story." I wanted to rush out and flee into the great city of Rome.

Paul calmly leaned forward, placed his elbows on the table and interlaced his fingers, all the while, his deep-set, sharp, piercing eyes kept a steady gaze into mine. "We have plenty of time," he said and again he raised one eyebrow and tilted his head to listen.

I took a deep breath and began, leaving nothing out.

"Where's Pharaoh now?" Epaphrus questioned. "I remember that Philemon really loved that horse."

The stress had exhausted me. "May I have a drink?" I requested, lifting my hand to my head. My whole body had begun to tremble. "I believe my fever has come back and my head is hurting. He's with the um… um… the innkeeper in um…in Ephesus. He promised to k..."

I was stress, drained and resented telling these strangers what I had done. My head was pounding and my brain and mouth refused to cooperate. They all began to look like strangers and fear gripped me. My ears were ringing and their strange voices seemed very far away. I felt nauseous and my vision blurred. Who are these men? Perhaps one of them had hit me.

I broke into a very cold sweat. The room spun faster and faster, and grew darker and darker. Sounds became weaker and then far, far away, and...then… nothing.

I faintly heard my name and realized I was on the floor being held down by gentle but firm hands.

"Onesimus! Listen to me, Onesimus. You must have been hurt worse than we thought. We're your friends. Let us help you." I realized what Epaphrus was saying and quit struggling. With their help I managed to sit on the bench and lay across the table. My ears were still ringing and I still felt nauseous.

"You've been delirious, Onesimus, and have been fighting us, all of us," said Luke.

"You thought I was the man who wounded and robbed you," said Tychicus with a friendly smile, "and you came for me. It took all of us to hold you."

Paul walked around the table and stood by me. "Onesimus," his voice sounded like thunder. "You are under the power of evil spirits from Satan! I command them all to come out of you in the Holy name of Jesus Christ." He poured olive oil in his hand and laid it on my head. I felt it running down my face and into my ears. Some of the oil made a path down my nose and dropped onto my hand. My mind was in a painfully confusing whirl and I wanted to scream. Again Paul spoke, using a commanding tone, "In the Holy name of Jesus Christ." Now there was no pain, and it felt like a fire burning on my head, followed by something that felt like cold water pouring over my entire body. I heard Paul speaking to me again. "We know there is no healing in the oil, Son. It is only a type of the healing virtue of Jesus Christ."

He laid both hands on my head again and said in a gentle, loving voice, "There are no more evil spirits in you, Onesimus. I command you to be perfectly healed from all the wounds you received. I command it in the name of our resurrected Lord and Master, Jesus Christ."

The Apostle Paul moved his hands from my head and smiled. Until that moment I cared little, if anything at all for these Christian men. I regarded them as simple fanatics, like the Essenes or the Zealots, except that these Christians seemed to be harmless.

I suddenly had a new feeling for them. Paul spoke to me again. "Believe that Jesus Christ is the resurrected Lord and Savior, and that he is the Son of God, and you will receive forgiveness and deliverance from all your sins." I felt what I later learned was the power of God in his words.

"I want to believe," I managed to say.

"Then kneel down, right here and now, and ask Him," said Luke. "Just confess your sins. Ask Jesus to forgive you and believe that he cares for you."

Tychicus and Luke knelt by my side and began to pray for me to believe on Jesus and be saved. I looked from one to the other for a moment before I realized they were praying for me, for my salvation. I heard my own voice actually praying for the Lord Jesus Christ to forgive all my sins. I don't remember just what I said, but I knew deep down inside that I had touched the heart of Jesus and that God, his Father, had forgiven my sins, though I had trouble understanding how.

I began to laugh, but it was the laughter of joy, real joy, a kind that I had never experienced before; I cried, but the tears were tears of happiness.

"Thank God," I cried, "I'm one of them now!" They all knew what I meant. We laughed and rejoiced together. Suddenly a terrible thought seemed to overshadow and destroy all my new joy. I turned to Paul and said, "But I'm a thief! How can I be a Christian?"

"You've already become a Christian," Paul assured me. "When you repented of your sins, God forgave them because Jesus paid your debt for sin when he died on the cross for all sin. That included your being a thief! God will work his will in your life from this moment forward unless you rebel against his plan for your life."

"Must I return to Master Philemon and be a slave for the rest of my life?" I asked.

"You must return to your Master Philemon," the apostle said with finality. With Paul's words, my heart sank. Now I could not continue my search for Martha or practice medicine. Heavy silence filled the room and they all looked at me as if they expected me to say something, but I just soberly nodded my head in pensive understanding. It was the right thing to do.

After a very long silence, Apostle Paul asked, "Onesimus, would you like to stay with me and help in my ministry? Since you speak and write in most languages you could be of great service to me."

My mind was in a whirl. How could I make a decision so quickly when the consequences were so far reaching? And if I have to go back to Philemon, how could I stay here to help Paul?

"You'll have great opportunity," Paul continued, "you'll be able to use your skills as a physician, just as Luke does. What do you think?"

"But what about Master Philemon and his gold I stole, and his great horse?"

"Luke, bring me pen and ink and a scroll," Paul requested.

Luke placed a small table before the great Apostle and then the writing materials. From where I sat, it was easy to read what he wrote. It began:

> *I Paul, a prisoner of Christ, and Timothy our brother, unto Philemon, our dearly beloved and fellow laborer, and to our beloved Apphia and Archippus our fellow soldier, and to the church in thine house: Grace to you, and peace, from God our Father and the Lord Jesus Christ. I thank my God, making mention of thee always in my prayers, hearing of thy love and faith, which thou hast toward the Lord Jesus, and toward all saints; that the communication of thy faith may become effectual by the acknowledging of every good thing which is in you in Jesus Christ. For we have great joy and consolation in thy love, because the bowels of the saints are refreshed by thee, brother.*
>
> Wherefore, t*hough I might be much bold in Christ to enjoin thee that which is convenient, yet for love's sake I rather beseech thee, being such an one as Paul the aged, and now also a prisoner of Jesus Christ I beseech thee for my son Onesimus, whom I have begotten in my bonds.*

When I read these words I was struck with amazement. To think that the great Apostle Paul would claim me as his son in the Lord! Tears of love and gratitude flowed down my cheeks unchecked. I arose and stood behind Paul and read swiftly until I caught up with his writing.

> *Which in times past was to thee unprofitable, but now profitable to thee and to me: whom I have sent again. Thou therefore receive him, that is, mine own bowels: whom I would have retained with me, that in thy stead he might have ministered unto me in the bonds of the Gospel: but without thy mind I would do nothing; that thy benefit should not be as it were of necessity, but willingly. For perhaps he therefore departed for a season, that thou shouldest receive him forever; not as a servant, but above a servant, a brother beloved, especially to me, but how much more unto thee, both in the flesh, and in the Lord? If thou count me therefore a partner, receive him as myself.*
>
> *If he hath wronged thee, or owe thee ought, put that on mine account; I Paul have written it with mine own hand. I will repay it.*

At this point, I interrupted Paul's writing. I fell on my knees before the distinguished Apostle of Christ. "You can't do this for me," I cried. "I'm not worthy. I'll find some way to repay this debt myself." I put my face in my hands and wept bitterly before them all.

Paul placed a hand under my chin and raised my head until I could look him in the eye.

"Look at me, Onesimus," he said. "You are now as worthy as an angel of God, yet it is good that you feel unworthy. If Philemon will send you back to help in my ministry, you will be worth more than all the gold you took. You'll repay the debt by working with me."

I stood and he continued writing:

> *...albeit I do not say to thee how thou owest to me even thine ownself besides. Yes, brother, let me have joy of thee in the Lord: Refresh my bowels in the Lord. Having confidence in thy obedience I wrote unto thee, knowing that thou wilt also do more than I say But withal, prepare me also a lodging: for I trust that through your prayers I shall be given unto you.*
>
> *There salute thee Epaphrus, my fellow prisoner in Christ Jesus; Marcus, Aristarchus, Demas, Lucas, my fellow laborers. The grace of our Lord Jesus Christ be with your spirit.*
>
> *Amen*

Paul gave the letter to Luke, asking that he copy it for his records.

Too overwhelmed to speak, I sat thinking. This is indeed the greatest love that has ever come into my life. It is as great as the love of my own mother, and much greater than the love Master Mamun had for me. This must be the love of Jesus Christ demonstrated through men.

I laid my quill beside the inkpot and rubbed my hand across my tired eyes. I'm growing weaker daily and I certainly can't write anymore today. My distended abdomen is feverish and I can no longer straighten myself. Martha sees my agony, but we both know there is nothing we can do.

I miss my sweet mother. She always made me feel better. She died some years ago, but thank God, she died in the Lord.

With great effort I pulled myself up to go in for the day, but before I had taken my first step, Sarah was by my side. "Here, Papa, lean on me," she said. As we reached the door, a whiff of fresh meat roasting over open flames, filled my nostrils.

"Oh, my little one," I said, seeing Tychicus. "You're growing so fast and learning something new every day. It hurts to realize I will never be able to take you hunting and do all the other things a grandfather does with his grandson, but I know that your father will see that you have all the love and teaching you need."

As I lay down to rest, he snuggled close to me. Our sleep was peaceful.

Each man set about his task, silent in his own thoughts. Epaphrus was busy preparing food and singing a song about Jesus. I heard him sing it before, but now I understood it and a strange new joy came over me.

Breaking the long silence I said, "I still want to find Martha. You may think that I'm a fool to say that I'm in love with her since I've seen her only once, when their wagon wheel broke, but, that once was all it took for me to know."

"I know Martha and her Uncle Abraham," Tychicus said casually. "Apostle Paul once worked making tents and repairing ship sails with Brother Abraham."

Dumbfounded, I wheeled around. Tychicus continued preparing the vegetables as though he had said *'It's a nice day.'*

"What did you say?" I demanded, in anger.

Tychicus glanced up and smiled "I know Mar..."

"You knew I was looking for her," I interrupted with anger, "and did not tell me that you know her?" Confusion quickly begun to replace my anger. "Why?"

Tychicus laid down his work and stepped closer to me. "Onesimus," he spoke in a fatherly tone, "you were a person full of unclean spirits…a runaway slave…a thief! If you had not accepted Christ as your Savior, we would have done everything in our power to keep you away from Martha."

"We?" I questioned with emphasis. "We? All of you know her?" I asked, even more confused.

"Martha is a fine Christian woman and her uncle has given much to the church. Because of that he's been greatly persecuted by the Zealots and others, but…" a big smile brightened his face, "things are much different now. You're a new creature in Christ!" His statement was almost like a happy song.

I sank onto the wooden bench feeling drained. "You're right. I'm still not worthy of such a wonderful woman, but…" my choking emotions stopped me from speaking.

Tychicus patted my shoulder and with twinkling eyes said, "I'll take you to her first thing in the morning."

Paul had been sitting silently listening. "Remember," he said, "you are to take my letters to the churches at Ephesus and Colosse the first of next week, and you, Onesimus, will take my letter to Philemon."

"I'll make preparations first thing in the morning," said Luke.

"I'm glad Onesimus is going with me," said Tychicus.

The next morning I was up early, nervously waiting for Tychicus to get ready.

Once on the road, I had to step swiftly to keep up with him. Little was said as he led me along the eastern bank of the Tiber until he crossed the old Aurelian road between the river and the Palantine Hill where the Imperial Palace stood. We then took a road that curved around the Aventine Hill and went past the Avernal Gate. Soon we came to a road that went south for several hundred yards and ended at the gate of a lovely home. Tychicus pushed it open and we walked into a small fenced yard filled with colorful flowers. The house was old but in good repair. There was a well close to the door. Everything was so quiet that the only sound seemed to be the buzzing bees and my pounding heart.

An elderly servant answered his knock "Come in, Master Tychicus. My Lord will be glad to see you."

As we entered the room an old man came forward and embraced Tychicus.

"Abraham, this is Onesimus, a newcomer to the faith. Onesimus, meet Brother Abraham, Martha's uncle."

I offered him my hand but he ignored it and embraced me as he had Tychicus.

"Welcome, Onesimus," he said with a slight bow.

"Thank you, Brother Abraham." I was trying to adopt that Christian custom of calling another Christian 'brother' as quickly as possible.

We sat on a long divan and the servant brought cool grape juice in tall slender glasses. After such a long walk it was satisfying. Through an open door I saw three shelves with reading material and a table with a vase of lovely flowers. I wondered if Martha had picked them.

Abraham and Tychicus were discussing our journey next week.

"Is Martha here?" Tychicus finally asked.

"No, she's visiting her cousin in Ostia and will not return until Tuesday."

My heart seemed to drop into my sick stomach.

Tychicus was saying, "Onesimus and I must leave early next week but we do want to see her before we go."

"Onesimus!" Brother Abraham exclaimed. "I've heard Martha mention that name many times since she's been here. Are you the doctor who set my grandson's arm?"

"Yes," I nodded.

"She'll be very disappointed if she doesn't get to see you."

"She won't be disappointed," I assured him. "I won't leave Rome until I've seen her."

"But," Tychicus said, "Luke is making arrangements for us to sail early next week. It may be two or three weeks before another ship leaves. We must go next week."

"Tychicus," I said with firmness, "I've gone through far too much to see her and I won't go until I do."

"Well," he said thoughtfully, "I know Paul is eager to get those epistles delivered but I'll try to get at least one more week. Perhaps by that time Martha will be back."

"Thank you, Tychicus," I said with visible relief.

While the older men continued their visit, my mind was on Martha.

Soon we were on the long walk back to Paul's house, but my heart was light with hope.

As we entered, Paul was praying and we joined him. I thanked my newfound God for letting me find Martha.

When he had finished, Paul asked, "Well, did you see her?"

"No," I replied sadly, "she's visiting a cousin in Ostia."

"Um," Paul frowned, "what a disappointment!"

"She won't be back before next Tuesday," explained Tychicus, "and we really need to leave for Ephesus before that."

"I can't go until I've seen her," I declared. "I must find out if she'll marry me."

"How do you plan to take care of a family?" Paul questioned "You are still a servant, and there is a chance that Philemon may not agree to let you come back to help me. There's also a chance that he won't let you marry. Have you forgotten that he owns you and your future?"

"But Philemon is your friend," I argued, "and I can only hope that he will let me come back."

"As a new Christian, you must learn to trust God in all matters. Ask him to take complete control of your life and work it out according to his will," instructed Tychicus.

"Good advice," added Paul. "God knows what's best for you and Martha."

Wanting to be alone for a while I walked aimlessly out of the house and started up the road. The dream about my mother flashed into my mind. I have certainly suffered physically, and now this heartache is worse than being hit over the head. Without Martha I feel I will never be happy. I want to place my life in God's hand, but how does one do that? I heard myself say aloud, "Martha, I must at least talk to you!"

I continued walking, letting my thoughts flit haphazardly until I realized I was near Haggai's Inn, so I decided to spend the night.

Surprised, Haggai stretched out his arms and cried, "Where have you been? I've asked everyone if they've seen you, but no one remembered seeing you for days!"

I sat at the table with him and told him all about my attack and my recuperation, but I didn't tell him about becoming a Christian.

"Onesimus," Haggai said in a low voice, "I think I saw your dagger only last night. A man came in here with that Jehu. You remember him, don't you?"

"Yes," I replied.

"Well, a man with Jehu had a dagger exactly like yours. I didn't think much about it then, but it had a thin double-edged blade about twelve inches long. The scabbard was hand-tooled with a flower on it."

"That sounds like mine," I agreed. "Old Elias made it for me. Is that man still around here?"

"I hadn't seen him before, but if he's taken up with Jehu, he'll be back. Jehu has been coming often just because I told him I don't want him here. He looks for trouble. He meets others of his kind here and they have long talks."

"I'm weary and need to go to my room, but if either of them come back, let me know at once."

In my room I found everything as I had left it. There were some coins, more than I remembered leaving. *This will be enough to buy food and lodging for several months. I will spend it wisely and make it go as far as possible*, I thought.

After spreading my sheepskin, I was soon asleep.

Early the next morning I ate a good breakfast then rented a horse. At Paul's house, I dismounted, tied the horse to a tree and filled a bucket with water for him before going inside.

Paul smiled as I entered. Everyone was there except Epaphras. I expected the usual, 'Where have you been?' but no one said a word. I sat at the table.

"That's a fine looking horse," Apostle Paul remarked "Is he yours?"

"No, Mas… Brother Paul," I replied. "I rented him." Remembering I had come to them broke, I told them of the coins I had left at the inn and suddenly realized that they were not mine to purchase food or lodging. "Since you promised to pay Philemon the money I owe him, I want to give these to you." I held out the coins.

"Just keep them, Onesimus," the Apostle replied. "You will need money for your journey back to Colosse."

"Thank you, Mas… Brother Paul. You're very kind but I cannot leave Rome until I have seen Martha." It was hard to try to break the life-long pattern of calling a superior, master.

"I got permission from my Roman guard for Epaphras to go to Ostia and bring Martha home before you leave," Paul said.

"But…Brother Paul, I'm not…but why do this for me? I don't deserve it."

"I guess that's why. If you were to think of yourself more highly than you ought, I would treat you differently. You see, I know that I am the most unworthy apostle in Christ because I persecuted the Church of God."

"I don't understand. I have been told by many people that you are the greatest apostle."

"Before I met the Lord Jesus on the road to Damascus, I persecuted the Christians, even unto death. I also gave my consent to the stoning of Stephen. So you see, son, I ***am*** the most unworthy of all."

I sat in awe before this great, humble man. The room was full of power that seemed to demand silence and worship of God in the Spirit. These feelings were so new to me, so overpowering! I sat with my head bowed until he spoke again.

"You'll be able to see Martha, but be prepared to go back to Philemon with Tychicus."

"I'm ashamed to see him. I've treated him so badly," I admitted. "I'm also afraid. He could have me executed for stealing his horse and gold, and running away."

"Philemon is a Christian. He will do what is right, but you must be willing to abide by his word for your future."

"And," Tychicus added, "a part of being a Christian is learning to trust your life to God."

After a little while, I thought about Jehu and his renegade friend. If I could get the law to search them, I just might get some of the gold back. I felt sure the newcomer had led me into that shack and Jehu struck me. How strange that I would think of the law. Before my conversion, I would have gone after them myself and... Well, the Christian spirit was definitely working in me.

"Brother Paul," I said, "I'd like to stay at the inn for a couple of days, but I'll see Martha as soon as she returns, and I'll be here to go with Tychicus when he sails."

"God go with you, my son, but be careful of the Roman law. They'll do little to help you regain your gold."

I looked at him in amazement. How did he know what I was planning? A little shiver akin to fear ran down my spine.

"Thank you," I said and walked toward the horse.

I returned the horse to the stable and went into the inn. Haggai was busy so I sat down to a spicy meal. A few minutes later we were alone and Haggai sat at my table to rest for a minute.

"Have you seen either of them?"

"Yes, Jehu and that rascal were in the market place, and he still had your dagger in his girdle...in plain sight!"

"Do you know any of the Roman officers here?"

Haggai scratched his head. "None that I'd trust."

"Maybe I could get an officer to find where they're staying at night and search them, or maybe have them searched the next time they come in here."

"No!" he ordered. "I don't want trouble with a Zealot! I would be a ruined man. We'll find out where they're staying and take it from there."

I remembered that I was a Christian and could not take the gold by force even if I knew they had it. If the law could not help me, they would just have to keep it.

"I'd rather get an officer to help so it would be legal."

"Say," he exclaimed, "I just remembered that a few years back I helped an officer who was in a bad spot. Actually, I saved his life. He said that if I ever needed a favor he'd help. His name is Tykner, but he's not on duty here any more. I'll ask around and try to find him."

"Great!" I exclaimed "Let's search immediately."

"No," replied Haggai, "I will have to do it alone. He does not owe you anything but if I say thieves have stolen from one of my guests, and they are ruining my business, then he will feel that he is doing it for me. See?"

"That makes sense," I answered. "By the way, I must leave here shortly after noon tomorrow. I have an appointment with a friend."

"Give me a written description of your losses and I'll give it to officer Tykner. I'm almost sure Jehu and his friends are the ones who robbed you and he might get some of it back for you."

I felt good about my new way of thinking. Rubbing my hand across my sheepskin, I then tucked it tightly under my chin. It felt good that night.

Chapter Nine

Finding Martha

I felt like singing as I walked toward Martha's house. I could feel my faith growing and wished I could have known Jesus years ago. Well, I have accepted him now and I'll serve him regardless of the cost. I know that is a serious commitment. Almost daily since being in Rome, I've heard of a Christian who was mobbed, or killed. Some were tortured publicly with both Jews and Romans participating. They had a common hatred for the Christians.

Epaphras said I should not walk in fear, but go where I needed to go. If asked about being a Christian, I should answer, I am freeborn Roman and I belong to God.

When I turned down the road to Brother Abraham's house I met Epaphras. I hurried toward him but he motioned me back. I waited for him to approach me. He made no attempt to greet me as a Christian Brother, but stood a few feet from me and spoke in a low voice.

"Onesimus, there's a new wave of terrorism spreading against the Christians and the Jews. A Roman army suffered a terrible defeat in Africa, and many soldiers were killed. The priests of the idol temple say their gods are angry because Rome allows Christians to live. They blame us for defeat and are taking this opportunity to have us killed."

I started to speak but he stopped me. "We're being watched. Just as soon as you talk to Martha, go at once to the inn you told me about. Then, very early in the morning go by back roads to Paul's house." He hurried away.

As I slowly walked to the gate fear gripped my heart. Do the Romans know I'm a Christian? Am I leading them to Martha, causing her to suffer? I trembled as I lifted the latch.

A servant watching through the window opened the door. "Step in quickly."

It seemed my heart was in my throat as I entered. There stood Martha, more beautiful than I had remembered. I was struck dumb again so I held out two trembling arms. She ran into them and threw her arms around my neck. Pressing her to my breast, her warmth seemed to go through my entire body. I had not even imagined such ecstasy.

She pushed me gently away and said, "Oh, my dear Onesimus, I knew you would find me. I'm glad you're here. This sounds foolish, but when you sat on that wonderful horse, I knew I loved you. I've prayed daily that you would find me here in Rome. God has answered my prayer."

I took her by the shoulders and held her at arm's length. "Let me look at you. I never dreamed that love could be so wonderful. I want you to marry me, Martha." I held her close and kissed her again and again, feeling her warm lips returning my kisses.

She took my hand and led me to the divan. "Oh, Onesimus," she said as she sat close beside me, "I'm so glad you came when you did. If you had been an hour later you would have missed me."

"Why?" I asked.

Even now my uncle is getting everything ready to take us far away from Rome into the hills north of here."

"But, why?" I asked again, feeling foolish.

"There are two charges against us. We're Jews and we're Christians. The Romans are declaring death to all Christians so we must leave now."

"What are you going to do?" I asked.

"As soon as it's dark enough, we'll slip out the back way and go down the hill to a hole under the wall that's close to where Uncle Abraham is waiting for us with a small boat. We'll go up the river under the cover of darkness. He knows a way to get around Rome to a place where we'll be safe from this persecution."

"I'll go with you," I said. "I love you too much to lose you now."

"No," she said emphatically. "Brother Epaphras told me about your being a slave." Seeing my dismay she hurried on, "That makes no difference in my love for you, but it does make a difference in what you must do. You must return to Philemon as Brother Paul requested." She paused, and, seeing I was still stunned, she smiled and patted my arm. "Don't look so astounded, Onesimus. Epaphrus told me all about you running away, trying to find me, about you getting hit on the head and robbed, and about you becoming a Christian. Oh, Onesimus, I'm so happy!"

"Wonderful! But that leaves little for me to tell."

"You can always tell me of your love," she whispered. "I'll never get tired of that."

As I held her close and tenderly kissed her, the door opened and the servant said in a low, distinct voice, "My Lady, it's very late and your uncle is waiting. We must go at once."

We stood quickly and I embraced her again, reluctant to let her go. She pushed gently away. "Oh, Onesimus, I wish I could stay in your arms forever. Here..." she placed a folded piece of paper in my hand. "Uncle Abraham wrote out complete directions so that you can find us."

She placed a quick kiss on my lips, snuffed out the candle, and then was gone. The servant was gone, too, and I was left alone in dismal, lonely darkness. *Have I just found Martha to lose her again?* I questioned. Only the smoky smell of snuffed out candles told me this was real.

It was late. Time had passed swiftly. I ambled down the path, distraught at finding Martha just to lose her again, but now I knew she loved me and wanted to become my wife. I had held her in my arms and kissed her sweet lips. I felt her firm breasts pressed against me as she returned my kisses. I knew I'd lie awake for many nights, just reliving those exhilarating, tender moments.

I was so absorbed in thought that I walked a hundred yards past the inn before I realized it. I retraced my steps and walked into the dining room, and wondered if Haggai had located Officer Tykner. My mind was so filled with Martha that I could hardly make sense of anything. "Onesimus," I told myself, "Get your wits about you. You have much to do."

A tall candle burned on the table and another on a shelf, but the only sound I heard was a snoring guest. Going to my room, I quickly packed all my things and then went to sleep.

About an hour after midnight I was awakened by the sound of fast footsteps and then a voice. "Onesimus, get up. I have good news." I followed Haggai into the deserted dining room.

On a table were most of the things I had lost.

"Jehu and that partner of his had your stuff in a big strongbox. It had a basket over it and then piles of clothes and coats, but we found it!" he announced proudly, punctuating each of the last few words with a little tap on the table.

I looked with wonder. There was my girdle with its secret compartment where I carried the gold, and most of the gold was still in it. They had spent very little. I picked up my dagger and strapped it around my waist.

"How can I ever thank you for this?" I asked.

"You owe me no thanks," he replied. "I wish you could have seen their faces, especially their eyes when Officer Tykner and I stepped into the room. He flashed his sword and his heavy voice boomed, 'Get down, you wretches, on your bellies now!'" Haggai was flailing his slightly overweight arms dramatically as he related the events of the night. "They both fell on their faces with their hands behind them while he tied them."

"I wish I could have seen them," I responded with a big grin.

"While Tykner was tying them I examined that heap in the corner. On the very bottom we found your things. Jehu tried to tell him that those things belonged to him and his friend, but Tykner showed him the list you had written including the description of your dagger."

I took three pieces of gold from my girdle and offered them to Haggai.

"No, no," he said, holding both palms up between us. "I had more fun than I've had since I helped capture another band of cut-throats some years ago. Besides, with Jehu in prison, maybe the Zealots will stay away from my inn."

"Then let me pay you in advance for another month's lodging and food."

"Now that I will gladly accept," he said, and wrote a receipt. I heard him chuckling as he went to his own room and closed the door. Hurrying to my room I put my money belt underneath my clothes, rolled my other belongings in the sheepskin and put my dagger in my girdle. Only then did I remember that my sword was missing, but I was so happy to get the other things back that I felt no great loss.

I wrote a note telling Haggai that he was a wonderful friend and I would remember him as long as I lived, but I must now leave Rome. I left the note under a candlestick where he would be sure to find it and, hefting my pack, I stepped into the night and walked swiftly. Just as the shadows began to grow dim, I knocked on Paul's door.

"Who's there?" a voice called.

"Onesimus," I softly replied.

Tychicus opened the door. Luke and Epaphras were awake. We talked quietly so we wouldn't awaken Paul.

"Many of our people have been arrested," Luke said sadly.

"I suppose being a prisoner now is the safest thing that could happen to a Christian," said Epaphrus. "No one will search for us here."

"Brother Paul is considered a political prisoner, so he is safe for a while, but mark my words, his day will come," said Luke. "He will suffer greatly for the cause of Christ."

"How do you escape, Brother Luke," I asked. "You go from place to place without trouble."

"I'm a physician so I walk as a physician, carrying my bag of medicine. The people need me and I serve Christians and pagans alike, but I know that someday someone will point me out and say, 'There's one of them.' Then I will say, 'Yes, I'm a disciple of the Lord Jesus Christ.' I will never deny my Lord," he affirmed.

I slowly nodded my head, comprehending more and more what it meant to be a Christian.

"We'll stay inside, Onesimus, until time to board the ship," Tychicus said.

Paul began to stir as gleaming sunrays bounded through the tiny window. I unpacked my sheepskin and was soon asleep.

Breakfast brought a heavy silence. Everyone was thinking of the persecution raging outside our door. No Christian was safe unless he was already in prison.

I broke the silence. "The Lord has been so good to me. I regained most of the things I lost and I also saw Martha for a little while. She said she loves me and promised to be my wife."

"Splendid," Paul remarked, "Now you'll have plenty of money for your journey and enough to keep a wife for a while, but tell us more about your meeting with Martha."

I started to explain, "Ah, Martha! ..." I closed my eyes and momentarily forgot I was not alone. "She's so beautiful, and graceful, and I can still smell her special, delightful fragrance." I breathed deeply, my eyes still closed, and began to slowly turn around as though I was dancing. "And she was so soft and warm when she ran into my arms and lifted her beautiful face to me. We held each other so tightly that I felt her heart beat–and those lips…ah…" I slowly placed my fingertips on my lips, still remembering the feel of her gentle lips touching mine. "When our lips touched I felt like..." I suddenly realized where I was and what I was about to say, so I opened my eyes. Four grinning men were standing around me with arms folded. I started to stammer and blush and would have run out except the door was on the other side of the room. They all laughed, obviously sharing my joy as well delighting in my embarrassment.

Paul said, “Martha is a wonderful Christian.”

Luke slapped me on the back and then, with a little chuckle, he sat down and picked up a scroll.

“Brother Paul,” I said after a while, “I want to give the gold to you.”

“No, Onesimus. I wrote to Philemon that I would repay what you owed him. The fact that God has helped you regain what was stolen does not change that. You will need that and much more in the future.”

“You have my eternal gratitude,” I said as tears filled my eyes.

“What plans did you and Martha make?” he asked.

“She and her Uncle Abraham left last night for...”

“Yes,” Paul interrupted. “I helped Abraham make those plans, but where do you fit in?”

“I have a letter with a rough map telling me how to find their place, and if Philemon gives me permission to return, I’ll come by their home and hope to be married then. We didn’t have time to make definite plans. She just gave me this letter and then was gone.”

Another long silence was broken when Paul said, “Although I don’t know Philemon’s mind, I’m confident he will send you back. Certainly, you may go first and marry. Martha told me she loves you. You see, they are two of my closest friends and they’ve been here several times to visit.” After a long silence he continued, “When you are married it may be best that you leave Martha with her uncle and you can make their mountain home your headquarters. I feel every minister needs a wife.”

Silently choking back emotions, I made a mental note that the great Apostle Paul had called me a minister.

Chapter Ten

Going Back Home

The waves dashed high and some of them broke over the deck. The helmsman was strapped to the helm to keep from being washed overboard. The Captain ordered all sails furled except one that was necessary for proper steering.

As the ship rolled, I feared it would be destroyed but it always straightened in time to head into another wave. We were pounded for a day and a night.

Tychicus seemed as calm in the storm as he was in the sunshine, sleeping or studying, while I heaved and suffered.

After some time I crawled to where he sat reading and asked, "Don't you know we may be destroyed at any moment? How can you be so calm?"

He looked up with a wisp of a smile and said, "God rides in the wind, and we are His. My worrying can do no good." He went back to his reading.

I didn't know what time exhaustion finally drove me to sleep, but when I awoke the sun was shining.

Though still high, the waves were receding, so the Captain had ordered a few more sails hoisted and we were making better time. Within hours, the waves were calm enough that the Captain ordered all sails up and we moved swiftly across the water.

Tychicus was reading but I was sure that he had slept during the night. I arose and climbed to the top deck. The cool air refreshed me.

Tychicus came onto the deck and I followed him to the dining room. He and the Captain tried to get me to eat but I couldn't. I walked to the rail and watched the waves and the birds and some kind of fish that kept jumping out of the water. All hands were busy patching sails, splicing ropes, and repairing hatches or other parts of the ship that had been damaged by the storm.

Finally, I went below and stretched out on my sheepskin to let my body recuperate.

Several hours later Tychicus awakened me. "You've eaten nothing since the storm. You must come to supper."

I followed him and was soon seated. The Captain came to our table and said, with a hint of a smile, "You seemed to have been a very sick man."

"Yes, Sir, very sick," I answered.

"Is this your first voyage?" he questioned.

"No, Sir I have sailed many times before but never in such a storm," I said.

"It was quite a blow," he agreed, "but I've seen much worse storms… much worse!"

"How did you keep afloat?" I asked.

"I did lose a ship to one storm and came near losing my life. I held onto a piece of the broken ship and managed to get to an island, but," he sadly shook his head, "I lost my crew…every one of them."

"After that," Tychicus said, "I think I would have become a farmer or a shepherd."

"Ah, my friend," the old Captain replied with a smile, "when the salt sea gets into your blood..." He spread his hands and with a shrug moved on to visit the guests at the next table.

The ship was charted to stop overnight at Syracuse on the Isle of Sicily, and then go to Phenice on the Isle of Crete. Having been blown far off course by the storm, however, the Captain decided to sail to Nicopolis in Achaia and then turn south to Phenice.

We landed at Nicopolis about midnight. A sailor told us there was a good inn near the docks, so we decided to go there for breakfast the next morning.

We slept late so most of the guests had finished eating when we arrived. The last guests left shortly after we were seated.

"I hope you will be pleased," said the host as he brought our food. "We've fed so many this morning that I'm afraid the best food is already served."

"I'm sure we'll be happy with what you have," Tychicus said.

"I'll be happy to give you extra servings," the host continued.

"Thank you, but this will be plenty," replied Tychicus "It looks good to me."

"I agree," I said. "We've just sailed through a severe storm. Any food served at a table that is not rocking looks great."

"Then you've come from Rome?"

"Yes," Tychicus answered.

After serving our food, the host made a sign on the bottom of the platter from which he had taken our food.

When Tychicus whispered, "Maranatha," the gentleman smiled broadly and sat down at our table. Except for the three of us, the room was empty.

"Is the persecution very bad in Rome?" he asked.

"Yes," Tychicus affirmed, "and it's growing worse daily. The pagan priests claim the Roman army was defeated in Africa because the gods are angry that they let Christians live. Those pagans are trying desperately to bring about our destruction."

"I hear," I added, "that Nero orders the Christians to be persecuted to gain favor with the people."

"I was afraid of that," the host said, "but I lost a son in that campaign and I know that no Christian was to blame. He was a good Christian himself and a good soldier."

We expressed our sorrow for his loss then fell silent. Finally, when we were almost finished eating, the host asked, "Are you fleeing persecution?"

"No," Tychicus replied, "we are both on business errands."

"I remember you now," the host said suddenly. "You were in this very room with the Apostle Paul when he passed through on his way to establish a church in Ephesus." Then turning toward me he said, "You were not with them. Are you also a disciple?"

"Yes, he is," Tychicus answered for me, "and it's for Apostle Paul that we're making this journey. We're taking his epistles to Ephesus and Colosse."

"Yes, Brother Paul is a great man of God," the host said. "I've been privileged to serve him several times in this very room."

We visited most of the day and returned to the ship in the afternoon, just before it was ready to lift anchor.

When we were settled in our room I said, "I know Maranatha means 'Our Lord cometh,' but what was the sign he made on that platter?"

Making the same sign to show me how, Tychicus said, "He made the sign of a fish, which we Christians have adopted to greet each other when there might be enemies about, or when we want to know if a person is a Christian."

"I have a lot to learn," I said as we settled down to sleep.

The next morning there was no land in sight except for an occasional island. I took a seat near the bow and began reading a scroll that Brother Luke had loaned me about treating certain skin diseases. I had read of rashes, hives, ulcers, and skin depressions, and this work offered treatments from herbs, roots, salts, and oils. I appreciated the chance to learn more about the skin, its diseases and treatments.

Trading between Rome and the cities that lay on the Aegean Sea was at an all time high. Our ship was loaded with crates, bags, boxes, and skins as businessmen traveled from province to province in their quest for wealth. I overheard the Captain say, "We are overloaded since I took on so much cargo at Nicopolis. I hope we have fair weather until I can unload some of it at Phenice."

The Captain used little sail power, due to the heavy load, and our progress was slow. We reached Phenice and unloaded a lot of cargo there. When we left, the ship rode much higher in the water and the Captain ordered full sail as we set out for Camirus on the Isle of Rhodes.

The Captain was well acquainted with the Aegean Sea and knew how to steer a safe course between the dozens of islands and bars that were on every side.

"If we were heavily loaded," he said, "we could not get through these shoals. I would have sailed southwest between Icaros and Samos, and that would have delayed us about two days in reaching Miletus."

"I hope we don't run aground on these shoals," I said.

"Not much danger of that," he said, "but I can't say for sure. Storms can shift the shoals and very often new shoals appear after a severe storm."

I noticed a sailor perched far out on the prow of the ship and another sitting astride the yardarm high up on the mast.

"The man up there on the yardarm," the Captain pointed, "can usually see the shoals better than the one on the prow."

"What do you do after dark?" I questioned.

"I keep two sailors casting the plummet line all through the night. They will call out if they find the water less than five fathoms deep."

"I hope it works," I said.

"It has always worked for me," the Captain said, "but there have been times I've dragged the keel on the bottom," he admitted.

We landed in Miletus late the next day and stayed on the ship that night. I wanted to be alone to figure how I should meet Philemon. I was afraid of him, and also very ashamed. What about old Elias, or Cephas, or John who had been such a good friend. How would they receive me? Would they receive me at all? Paul's confidence that Philemon would give me freedom was a comfort, but I could still hear Philemon's words when I asked to go to Ephesus and establish a medical practice. '*You belong to me! I bought you with my gold!'* It was difficult to think he would ever sign my manumission papers.

I wanted to go back to Paul for several reasons. I would have my freedom, I would marry Martha, I could practice medicine, and I could help the great apostle in the work of the Lord. I was feeling a spiritual call to the ministry, and that gave me a certain hope that God would work his will in my life. Nevertheless, I trembled at the thought of standing before Philemon.

About midnight Tychicus saw that I was awake and restless and said, "We'll be carrying much less cargo on the return trip so we should make it much faster." He wanted to draw my mind away from my trouble.

"I may not be making the return trip," I said quietly.

"I believe you will," he answered. "Philemon is a great friend of Paul's, and he'll do all he can to promote the Gospel. What greater thing could he do than to send you back to work with him?"

"I do want to go back," I said.

"Paul really needs you," reasoned Tychicus. "Several have deserted him and returned to their old jobs, and I'm afraid that Demas will leave him soon."

"I would never desert him," I promised.

"I feel certain you will be returning with me, so now, go to sleep and quit worrying."

"But, even if I do return, I will go see Martha first so we will still go our separate ways," I reminded him.

"We'll work out the details later," he said as he lay back on his bed. Then, after a moment he added, "Where did Martha say they were going?"

"Abraham's letter said they would go far north of Rome into the mountains, about ten miles south of Perugia, and about fifteen miles west of the Tiber River," I explained.

I went to sleep thinking of Martha's warm kisses.

We left Miletus late that day and sailed west until we came to the strait between the Isle of Samos and the mainland. We landed in Ephesus late the next day. Tychicus went directly to the home of the elder to deliver the letter from Paul, and I went to the inn where I had left Pharaoh, going first to the stable. When he saw me, he began pawing the ground and prancing about. I went into the stall and putting my arms around his neck I wept for joy. This great horse had been more than a friend and I dreaded to think that I would have to leave him behind if Philemon sent me back to Paul.

I led him out of the stall and mounted him without saddle or bridle, just the hackamore that he wore most of the time.

As soon as we were out of the city, I touched his flank with my heel and he stretched out and headed for the foothills of the nearby mountains. About three miles out we stopped and I rested on a rock while he grazed. Finally he came and nudged me gently.

"Well, old boy," I said, "are you ready to run again?"

He pushed me off the rock. Laughing, I swung astride him and headed back to the inn. Before I went inside I put him in the stable and gave him a good rub down.

Plautus met me with joy. "It's good to see you, Onesimus."

"And I'm happy to see you, Plautus," I replied. "How have you been?"

"I've been well, but I've worried about you. I feared you might be caught in one of these terrible storms we've been having lately."

"We did run into a bad storm, but we managed to escape with only minor damage to the ship and sails."

"That's good," he said. "Hey, I saw you riding away on Pharaoh a while ago."

"He's as frisky as ever," I smiled. "I can see you've taken good care of him."

He nodded. "I've ridden him often to keep him in shape. You know, I felt like a king the first time I sat on him."

"I know the feeling," I agreed. "Thank you so much for caring for him. Oh, by the way, can I have my old room tonight?"

"Certainly," he said as he got up and opened a closet. "Here are all the things you left. I've tried to take good care of them, too."

I suddenly became aware of hunger pangs. "What's for supper?" I asked.

"When I saw you ride off, I sent the lad to the market for a nice big fish, and it's waiting for you."

I smiled, pleased that he remembered how I like fish, and headed for the dining room.

I enjoyed three days at the inn, taking long horseback rides, eating good food, and engaging in long talks with Plautus, while Tychicus handled church business for Apostle Paul. I rode over the city and visited the Jewish synagogue. I also visited the temple dedicated to the goddess Diana. The priests of Diana had several booths spotted about the city where they sold small gold and silver statues of the famous goddess.

"One day," I told myself, "Jesus Christ will return and these idols will be destroyed. No one on earth will worship any god except the one and only Jehovah, God and Father of our Lord Jesus Christ."

I wanted to tell them about the great joy this brought to me but I knew I was not capable of explaining it as the apostle had told me. I rode back to the inn with my heart overflowing with gratitude for the changes God had made in my heart.

That evening we were sitting by the fire. "Onesimus, you haven't mentioned Martha," Plautus remarked. "Have you given up on finding her?"

"I found her in Rome," I joyfully reported, "and as soon as I take care of some business matters, we plan to be married."

Plautus laughed happily, then after slapping me on the back, he returned to his work.

A sharp pain bent me over with sudden force. I thought I would try to write, but for the last few days I have been unable. I am confident though that God will give me the strength to finish my story.

It has been a great joy to hold my grandson. He has added fullness to my life that I would never have experienced without him. Sarah is a splendid mother, and, of course, no grandmother could be more wonderful than Martha.

Jacobus has been spending a lot of time with me lately. God has blessed him with a spirit of love for the lost and his call to the ministry has become the driving force in his life.

That night I lay down to sleep, thanking God for my wonderful family.

The next morning I called, "Jacobus."

"Yes, Papa." He came to me.

"I want to write, Son. I feel an urgency to finish."

"Are you sure you feel up to it, Papa?" Sarah questioned.

"I think so, Sarah, and I also need the fresh air. I'll be fine."

Martha observed it all without speaking, but smiled when our eyes met.

Jacobus helped me to my feet and walked with me to my table. The sun filtered through the leaves of the mammoth old tree that sheltered the entrance to our cave, and danced on our faces.

"Do you have enough ink and papyrus, Papa?" he asked.

"There is plenty for now, Son. I don't figure I'll need too much more."

Tychicus rented a horse and I rode Pharaoh. Because I dreaded the inevitable meeting with Philemon, I was in no hurry to travel the one hundred thirty miles. We asked the innkeeper each night how far it was to the next inn, and adjusted our speed accordingly. We rode into Philemon's place and stopped at the big house just before dark on the sixth day.

Old Elias was standing at the gate. I dismounted and stood, head bowed, before the old servant who had been like a father to me. Tychicus rode on to Philemon's house.

"Onesimus," he said, taking me by the shoulders. His old voice trembled with emotion as he said, "I knew you'd come back. Come on in and see the others."

I followed the old man, wondering why he did not at least chastise me as he had in the past when I did wrong. The servants gathered round me, shaking my hand and patting me on the back. Two of the old women kissed me as they cried for joy. Instead of receiving me like a criminal, they treated me like a brother. Overwhelmed, tears rolled down my cheeks.

Soon the truth struck me. I was yet to stand before Philemon! I figured they knew what he would do, and they felt sorry for me. He would probably give me the maximum beating allowed for a slave, and then perhaps he would sell me to be sent far away among strangers. I might never be able to see Martha again. By law, Philemon could have me executed for stealing his horse and gold. Fears tempted me to dash out the door, mount Pharaoh, and flee to some unknown place, but I remembered that I was a Christian, and my life was in God's hands. A sweet peace settled over me as I walked out on the porch and sat down.

In a few minutes I saw Philemon and Tychicus coming and stepped off the porch to meet them. I stood trembling before Philemon with my head bowed in shame. I was his slave. When I was a small lad in Egypt I saw a slave beaten to death for stealing. I could hear his terrible screams as the lash fell on his bloody body. Would Philemon have me beaten, or turn me over to the law to be hanged?

The moments felt like hours that Philemon did not speak. My eyes seemed to be glued to the ground and my chest ached with terror as the screams of a past memory whirled in my head. I dared not move.

"How are you, Onesimus?" I heard Philemon's caring voice; but surely my mind was playing tricks on me. His *face–I must look at his face*, I thought*, to know if I heard kindness in his voice.*

I lifted my eyes and found that he was gazing straight at me. He had a sad smile on his face, and there was compassion in his eyes.

With great humiliation I tried to answer but my words were choked. I sank to my knees with my face in my hands, weeping uncontrollably, but managed to brokenly say, "Master, I…I'm so sorry!"

Elias came and put his arm around my shoulders. "He'll be all right in a little while, Master."

With a sudden burst I wrapped my arms around Philemon's legs. "Master, I'm truly sorry. I beg you to forgive me. I've been so wrong."

"Tychicus told me a little about what has happened, but I'll hear it all from you tomorrow. It's good to have you with us again. Just get a good night of rest." He and Tychicus walked slowly back to his house without looking back.

Elias asked one of the young men to care for the horses and another to bring my things in, but I stayed on my knees and soon found myself alone.

"Dear God," I began to pray, "is it possible that you have taken control of my life?" I whispered aloud. "After all the wrong I did, please help me to make it up to Master Philemon and all my friends I let down, and I will give the rest of my life to serve you."

I got to my feet and went into the big house where there was an air of happiness and joy. After a terrific meal and long hours of conversation, I wrapped myself in my sheepskin and slept until the first morning light.

"Onesimus," Elias called when he heard me stir. "The master wants you to have breakfast at his table this morning so you better hurry."

I poured cold water into a basin. "I never saw the inside of the master's house all the time I lived here," I said aloud as I dried my face. Then turning to Elias I requested, "Will you go with me?"

He nodded and led the way. I stepped up by him and walked in silence to the gate near the front door.

"Go knock," he instructed. "I know how you must feel but you must act as though you belong there." He walked away and I stood there with my heart pounding in apprehension.

I did not recognize the lad who answered my knock.

"Come on in, Onesimus," Philemon called from another room.

I followed the lad to the dining room that was almost filled. Philemon sat at the head of the table and Tychicus was on his left. Archippus was at the far end and a man I did not know sat next to him. There were twelve persons in all, some I had never met but others I remembered.

"Sit here, Onesimus." Philemon pulled out the chair to his right.

I felt uneasy as Archippus glared at me. "I see the prodigal has returned. I hope you've learned your lesson," he snarled.

"I have learned many lessons, Master Archippus," I answered, "and I feel I will profit by them." I was determined that he would not provoke me.

"Philemon," Tychicus said, "Onesimus has an interesting story."

"I'm sure he has," he said. "I'll hear his story as soon as we've finished eating."

Remembering Elias' counsel, I ate as though I belonged there, speaking little but listening carefully as the others talked.

As the meal was finished, most of the men excused themselves until only Philemon, Tychicus, Archippus, and I were left at the table.

"Well, Onesimus, tell us." Philemon leaned back in his chair and waited for me to make sense of the terrible things I had done.

I took my time and told everything in detail. Then I came to the part about becoming a Christian and tears welled in my eyes. I continued on about how I found Martha and about our betrothal.

"Now Paul has sent me back to you," I said as I took his letter from my girdle and handed it to Philemon. "He asked me to deliver this to you."

"I'm delighted to hear that you're a Christian," he said as he took the letter and began reading. Everyone was silent as he read.

"Onesimus, have you read this?" he questioned.

"Yes, Master. I stood at Apostle Paul's side as he wrote it."

Philemon sat quietly staring at the parchment, and then said, "This will take a lot of study. Go back to the big house. I'll call for you when I'm ready to discuss it."

I walked down the dusty path with a heavy heart. Elias was eager to hear what had happened so I related it as best I could.

"Master Paul actually promised to repay Master Philemon for the gold you stole?" he questioned with astonishment.

"Yes," I answered, "but he said that I would be worth more than that if Master Philemon would let me come back to help him in his ministry because I know several languages and I'm young and strong. I'll just have to wait on Master Philemon's decision now."

The day seemed like the longest day I had ever spent. There was no word from the Master.

I wanted to sleep over Pharaoh's stall that night, but Elias had already spread my sheepskin. "You may sleep here tonight, Onesimus."

Even after I lay down, Elias kept asking questions, and I was glad for the chance to talk about becoming a Christian and about Martha.

Someone came into the big house and heard me talking. "Is that you, Onesimus?" he called.

"Yes, but who…John, is that you?" I asked as he made his way toward me.

"I had to come for supplies and since it's so late I decided to stay here tonight."

"I'm glad you did. It's good to get a chance to see you and talk."

"You young men go ahead and catch up," said Elias. "This old man needs some sleep."

"It is really good to have you back. It seems like old times. Where have you been?"

"What do you think the Master will do to me?" I asked, disregarding his question. "I'm afraid."

Elias' deep breathing suddenly broke into a loud snore, so John lowered his voice.

He thought for a minute. "You're the first one to run away since the Master has become a Christian. He used to deal very harshly with runaway slaves. You are the first to return without being captured."

We again lowered our voices for fear of waking others. We talked of horses, and cattle, and sheep, and the wide-open ranges. I finally asked, "Have you had any more trouble with horse thieves?"

"No," he replied. "It's late and we both have a big day tomorrow so I'll see you in the morning." The next morning I wanted to ride Pharaoh over the hills as I used to, but Elias told me that Master Philemon wanted me to take breakfast at his house again. "You'd better get going or you'll be late."

"Thank you, Elias," I said. "I'll go, but I'd much rather eat here with all of you."

I walked up to Master Philemon's house and a young girl opened the door for me. Like me, she had been born into slavery. Her mother had served Master Philemon before she died. *This young girl will probably never know freedom*, I thought.

"Master Philemon is waiting for you in the dining room," she said as I walked past her.

Again, Philemon sat at the head of the table with Tychicus on his left. Archippus sat to the left of Tychicus, and again the Master told me to sit next to him. To my right sat Epaphroditus, who was on his way back to Rome, having been on a mission for Paul.

After thanksgiving, we began our breakfast. For some time everyone visited as they ate, then Philemon asked how Epaphrus was doing. Before being arrested, he had been their pastor. Paul managed to have him put in his own hired house instead of the prison.

"He's faring well," Tychicus replied. "He is kept with Paul in his prison house. Actually Epaphrus is more in Paul's custody than in the custody of the jailer. Paul has great influence and most of the officers respect him."

Archippus told Tychicus of several converts who had been added to the church since he was here. Then Tychicus told of spending three days with the brethren at Ephesus. "They greatly appreciated the epistle that Paul had written to them," he said.

"Archippus," added Tychicus, "here's a letter that I am to deliver to you for the Colossians."

"Thank you," he said. "I will receive this letter from Paul with great joy. The church here at Philemon's house will be delighted. Epaphrus actually went to Rome for this letter, but was arrested when he refused to bow down to the Roman ensigns. We are all praying for his release so he may return to us."

"I'm rather confident that both he and Paul will be released soon," said Tychicus.

"God be praised!" Philemon raised his hands in worship. Is there really hope that they'll be freed?"

"Yes, there is much hope, and Paul said that if the church will pray, he feels certain that God will answer.

"Then," Archippus said, "I'll ask all who will, to join me in a three day fast and we'll pray for their release."

"I, too, have a letter from Paul," said Philemon. "Onesimus brought it to me. I'll read it to you, brethren, and then I want your advice concerning it and the request Paul has made."

A silence fell over the room as Philemon began. Then he came to the request.

> *".. I beseech thee for my son, Onesimus, whom I have begotten in bonds:*
>
> *which in time past was to thee unprofitable, but..."*

As Philemon continued to read, my mind went back to the moments I stood beside Paul reading with gratitude and amazement.

When Philemon finished reading the letter, he took his napkin and dried the tears from his eyes. I wiped my blinding tears on my sleeve. There was a spirit of deep appreciation for the love that Paul manifested toward me, a servant who was so very unworthy.

Philemon looked at me. "Onesimus, do you have anything to say?"

"Master," I said in a nervous voice, "everyone knows I am guilty of many crimes and I'm worthy of death." I took a deep breath and tried to clear my trembling voice. "All I can do is beg for your mercy and await your decision." I dropped my eyes to my shaking hands.

"Do you want to go back to Paul?"

"Yes, Master, I do," I said without hesitation, "and I feel that God has called me to preach the gospel of Jesus Christ. I need to spend time with Brother Paul to learn from him. I am well learned in many subjects, but I know very little about the precious Gospel of Jesus Christ. Master, I'm committed to the will of God for my life, and I believe that you will be led by the Holy Ghost in your decision concerning me."

"You have spoken as a true Christian, Onesimus," Tychicus said. Then he addressed Philemon, "The Apostle Paul especially wants Onesimus because he is fluent in the languages that are necessary to get the Gospel to every nation, and also because he is a capable physician."

"It's certain that Onesimus has more talents than most men," Philemon said. "That's why it's hard for me to give him up. I had such high hopes for him, even after he ran away. I fear I may never see him again."

Silence again filled the room. I could feel my heart pounding. Finally Philemon asked, "What do you think, brethren? Shall I send him back to minister to Paul?"

"Philemon," Tychicus said, "Paul and I both feel that God has called Onesimus to his work. Some of Paul's workers have left him during the last few months, and it looks like Demas will leave also. Right now the persecution is severe. There is another matter I need to mention. Onesimus is in love with a wonderful Christian girl. She and her uncle, who has already given his blessings to their marriage, are well respected by the Christians in Rome. Paul is also in favor of this marriage. We request that you send him back to Paul, to his wife, to his future ministry of preaching and healing."

Philemon waited silently for the others to speak.

Archippus stared at me. "I realize that the final decision rests with you, Philemon, but you have asked for our thoughts. We all know that this slave has committed terrible sins, running away and stealing. I think he should receive punishment instead of a hero's welcome. I know that we've all sinned, but we have paid for them. I find no place in God's Word where God rewards evil, but He rewards us for good. The fact that Onesimus is well educated makes his crimes even more obnoxious." He looked from one to the other, expecting someone to agree, but it was obvious that no one else felt the same.

"Brethren," Epaphroditus said, "we were all sinners before we were forgiven by our Lord Jesus Christ. We were driven to do evil by the same spirits that drove Onesimus. We have been forgiven and are no longer guilty. Let us also remember that Brother Onesimus is no longer guilty. He is no longer a thief, but, as Paul said, a beloved brother. I feel we should forgive him just as the Lord has forgiven us, and send him back to Paul and to his betrothed."

Tychicus and Philemon nodded agreement but Archippus sat with a frozen countenance. It was evident that he wanted me to be punished for my sins.

Philemon stood. "Thank you, brethren, for your advice. It has been a great help. Archippus, you are right in your judgment, but you lack mercy and compassion. I feel we must love and forgive as Christ has taught." Then he turned to me. "Onesimus, tomorrow I will go before the Roman Consul in Colosse and give you your freedom. I will also see that you receive Roman citizenship at that time. You may return to Paul and be married."

Overwhelmed with gratitude, I could only weep as Philemon and the others embraced me in Christian love. Even Archippus embraced me and bid me God-speed.

"Master Philemon," I said in a broken voice, "only God knows how I appreciate what you are doing. I need all of you to pray that my life will count for God."

Chapter Eleven

Manumitted

I awoke to the odors of breakfast. The sound of stirring in the big house brought a strange new peace. Philemon had agreed to let me eat with the servants that morning.

After breakfast John and I walked to the stalls to saddle his horse.

"I thank God for you, Onesimus," he said. "We all hate to see you go, but we're glad for your sake. I hear you're getting married." His face spread in an oversized grin.

I nodded and beamed at the remembrance of Martha. "John, I'll never forget this place, nor will I forget Philemon, nor any of you. You will be in my heart as long as I live."

"I wish I could spend the day with you, but I have a lot of work to do." He mounted, and turning in the saddle, reached out his hand. "God go with you, Onesimus."

I grasped his hand and said, "And God go with you, my friend."

As I turned to the stable to check on Pharaoh, Tychicus joined me. "We need to make some plans."

We went outside to the shady side of the stalls and sat on two big rocks. "What do you have in mind?" I asked.

"Well," he said thoughtfully, "we don't have to be in too big a rush. Tomorrow is the Lord's Day so maybe we'll leave a couple of days after that. What do you think?"

"That sounds fine to me," I returned. "Will Epaphroditus go back to Rome with you?"

"He left before breakfast. No one but Philemon knew he was leaving."

"I had hoped he would go with us," I said.

"He likes to travel alone because he reads a lot and says he can't concentrate when others are around," he explained.

"I really do appreciate what he said in my defense to Philemon."

"So do I, but I felt confident about Philemon's decision from the start."

"I didn't have your faith," I admitted. "I was afraid Philemon would keep me here or sell me. I know that is what I deserved."

"Is Master Philemon still at the house?" I asked after we had talked for a while.

"No, he left when Epaphroditus did. He went to Colosse to attend some personal business and to bring back your writ of manumission and your Roman citizenship."

"All this seems like a dream," I said shaking my head.

"It's no dream," Tychicus answered, "but the greatest thing that's ever happened in your life. How does it feel to be really free?"

"I um…I…," I shrugged, stammering in a loss for words. Then with a strange outburst I confessed, "I desired it, prayed for it, feared it, and doubted it, and now that it's here, I'm terrified."

"Why are you afraid?"

"Well, I've made a lot of decisions but important decisions have always been made for me by my masters. Now, my entire future will depend on my own ability, and that's a heavy responsibility."

"You'll have no trouble," Tychicus assured me. "Just take everything as it comes, and pray for wisdom and guidance from the Holy Ghost."

"I'll always try to do that," I said as I stood. "I think I'll go pack my camp outfit and the few other things I have and be ready to leave."

Philemon returned mid-afternoon. He gave the reigns to the stable boy and called for me as he stepped into the big house. All the servants who were not busy crowded eagerly into the huge room. Tychicus and Archippus had come in with Philemon. Old Elias sat on a bench against the wall, and Cephas, who had been filling the water pots, sat beside him.

When Philemon went to the door leading to the dining room and turned to face us, everyone hushed in anticipation.

"Onesimus," Philemon began, "it is my pleasure to give you these papers of manumission, signed and sealed by the Roman Consul. You are a free man!" he said, beaming with happiness.

Wanting to share in my good fortune, the servants gathered around me for a few moments. They laughed and cheered, and patted me on the back.

After they quieted, I said, "Master Philemon, I thank God for you and for this day, and as I accept this writ of manumission, I acknowledge another servitude that is more important than any I have ever known. I'm not free, but I'm a servant of the Lord Jesus Christ." I stared momentarily at the precious paper in my hand, and then looking at Philemon, I continued. "Master Philemon, you have been the best and most generous master I have served. You won my love, even before I ran away. I will always love you and all these people, and this place. Thank you," I said, again wiping tears.

"We all love you, too, Onesimus, and here is a paper that will tell the world that you are a free Roman citizen. My joy seemed to overflow as I accepted my citizenship papers. Some of the servants crowded around to see what the two papers looked like.

"Onesimus," Philemon got my attention. "I have something else for you."

I noticed with confusion that he was holding another paper. What more could this gracious man do for one so undeserving? "This," he said, "is a bill of ownership for the big red stallion, Pharaoh. I gladly give him to you to use in service to the Apostle Paul."

Before I realized what I was doing, I knelt to express my gratitude. He took me by the arm. "Please stand up," he said. As I stood he placed the bill of ownership in my hand. "I appreciate your grateful attitude, but you must never bow to any man. Worship only God."

"But I'm so thankful, Master, and I do hold you in high honor."

Philemon smiled. "The Lord is your Master now. You need never call me Master again."

"You will always be Master Philemon to me," I said, "as well as a brother in Christ."

"When do you plan to return to Rome?"

"Tychicus and I plan to leave Monday. He will go directly to Rome, and I plan to go see Martha and hope to be married. Then I will do whatever Paul needs me to do."

"May God go with you, Onesimus." He hugged me, and then quickly left, but I glimpsed a tear in his eye.

The Lord's Day was of great interest to me. It was the first church service I had attended since becoming a Christian. They sang hymns, prayed, and Archippus preached a wonderful message about the Lord's return to earth. I was anxious to learn all I could about my new faith. Archippus was very learned in the Law and the Prophets, but I enjoyed the testimonies most. They told of God delivering them from numerous problems, and about being healed. I was sorry to hear the final 'Amen'.

Tychicus and I were up early Monday morning to leave without telling anyone except Philemon. Tychicus mounted the horse we had rented in Ephesus, and I rode Pharaoh. As we started out of the yard there went up a volume of voices bidding us farewell. It seemed that every person on Philemon's vast empire was there to tell us good-bye.

Seven days later, as the sun begun to set, we arrived in Ephesus. Tychicus had some time to spend with the elders in the church, and I enjoyed a wonderful three-day visit with Plautus.

Embarking on a large, three-mast ship that was used to transport soldiers and horses, I was pleased that Pharaoh would be cared for in his own private stall.

We landed first on Rhodes at Patara where the crew unloaded a lot of cargo and took on new passengers before sailing on to Caesarea. There they spent two days loading and unloading cargo and making repairs to the ship.

When we sailed for Alexandria in Egypt, the Captain said we would spend four or more days there.

In Alexandria, the Captain needed help with some papers written in Arabic and was very grateful that I could read them for him. "If I can ever help you, Onesimus, let me know."

"As a matter of fact, Captain, I may need your help here in Alexandria." I told him about my mother. "I must find her, and if I can't buy her, I will steal her and take her to Rome with me."

His eyes narrowed in momentary thought. "That would be a daring undertaking, however…" he paused again, stroking his bearded chin in serious thought, "…if you can get her aboard without the authorities knowing it, I'll take her to Rome."

"Well," Tychicus said as we walked down the street. "Aren't you glad we couldn't get a ship where you could have gone overland to Abraham's place?"

"Yes, in a way." We were yelling to be heard above the noise of the Alexandria streets. "I am determined to find Mother. I'll just have to trust God to help me."

"I'll do all I can to help, too," Tychicus said.

We rented a horse for Tychicus and rode to where Master Mamun had been my teacher for many years. Wonderful memories flooded my mind as I sat staring at the vacant old house, now in a state of ruin. I noticed that one of the old servant's houses was occupied.

"What do you want?" an old woman asked as she opened the door. Her face looked a little familiar, but I couldn't place her.

"I'm searching for the wife of the old Physician Mamun. Is she still in this area of the city?"

"She died a few months after the doctor did."

"What happened to the servant woman who took care of her?"

"Someone bought her and took her away."

"Do you know who bought her or where she was taken?" I questioned.

She shook her head.

"Do you know anyone who might know where she is?"

Again she shook her head and closed the door.

"I'm sorry, Onesimus," Tychicus comforted. "I know this is very painful, but God has a way of working things to your good."

We continued our search where I had known people when I lived here, and one of them remembered me, but could not tell me where my mother had been taken.

"I hope you will be able to find her, Onesimus," he said "We all loved her very much. She did all she could for all of us after Master Mamun died, but then she was sold."

As we left, I remembered another of Master Mamun's patients who lived in the edge of the city so we turned the horses in that direction.

He remembered me and seemed happy to see me again. "Yes, I saw your mother when she was sold but I did not know the man. I heard that he was an innkeeper somewhere here in Alexandria. That's all I can tell you. I was also there when the Doctor's wife died.

"Thank you," I said feeling a little more hope. "We'll go to every inn in this city until we find her."

"I hope you can find her. She's a good woman," he said as we rode away.

Darkness had fallen so we decided to spend the night at the first inn we found. The innkeeper knew nothing about Mother or Doctor Mamun.

The next morning we started our search, stopping at every inn we found. After an unsuccessful day, distraught and tired, we rode on to the next inn. As darkness again settled in I said, "If it's all right with you, we'll stay here tonight."

"That will suit me." Tychicus said. "I'm worn out." A lad took our horses to the stable. Then, taking our valuables, we headed inside. Securing a room we then went to the dining room for a very late supper. Throughout the meal, Tychicus tried to lift my spirits, but all he got was a faint smile. We were the last guests in the dining room. Seeing the servants coming in to clean we gulped down the last of our drink and started for our room.

"I believe," Tychicus said in a serious manner, "that we'll find her very soon. We have to keep our hopes up."

A young maid came in from the dining area and carried a heavy pot of water to an old servant who stood across the hall from our room with her back to us. She had a mop in one hand and now held the large pot of water in the other.

"Yes," he continued, "with God's help we will find her very soon, Onesimus."

When Tychicus said my name, the servant wheeled around. The pot she was holding hit the floor with a tremendous crash, breaking noisily, its many pieces scattering in every direction and spilling a soapy liquid over the floor. Her mouth seemed to be frozen in shock, and, as her hands flew high above her head, the mop catapulted almost to the ceiling. "Onesimus," she managed to say with a trembling voice. "My son, my son Onesimus!"

As my arms enveloped her, I realized how frail she had become. "Oh, Mother, I have missed you. Are you well?"

When we realized the water had run around our feet, we stepped clumsily backward, bumping into Tychicus. All three of us landed on the soapy, slippery floor, laughing noisily, while mother quickly slid off my good friend's lap into a massive puddle of water.

"Mother, meet Tychicus," I said from my seated position. "Tychicus, this is my mother, Hagar."

First to his feet, Tychicus took mother's hand and helped her up. "I am so proud to meet you. Onesimus is a great friend."

Just as I was getting up, the innkeeper came running in. He saw that the broken pot had spilled water over the floor, and the three of us stood hand in hand, laughing uncontrollably while dripping with water.

Having suddenly lost her gleeful countenance, Mother began to hurriedly pick up the mop and the broken pieces.

"What is the meaning of this?" he shouted. "Old woman, you are disturbing my guests. I'll have you beaten!"

I placed my arm around her trembling shoulders. "This old woman is my mother, Sir. I have been searching for her for many years. She will go to our room and stay there to visit tonight. Please send some drinks and fruit for us."

"Yes, my Lord," he answered with a livid scowl and a half-hearted bow, but his angry red countenance warned me that I had gotten off to a bad start with him.

Mother grabbed the mop and started to clean up the water. I called after the innkeeper, "Sir, please be kind and send someone to clean this water."

"Yes, my Lord," he hissed through closed teeth.

"Son, are you no longer a slave?" Mother asked as we went into the room.

"No, my dear Mother. I am a free Roman citizen"

"How did you get your freedom?" she asked in amazement.

The refreshments were delivered and we spent nearly half the night talking, sometimes laughing, and sometimes crying.

"I can't stay awake any longer," said Tychicus as he went to his mat in one corner. "Hagar, I am so pleased to finally get to know you. You have a fine son and I know you are very proud of him. I'll see you two in the morning." Very soon he was sound asleep.

"Do you have it easy here, Mother?"

After a moment she replied, "I have plenty to eat, but as you can see, I wear rags. He makes me do most of the dirty cleaning, and usually I have to work late into the night…like tonight. There is still another hour's work to be done."

"I'll buy you from him," I said. "I'm to be married soon and I'll take you to Rome to live with us.

Early the next morning I spoke to her master about buying her.

"Absolutely not," he answered emphatically. "She's a good scrub woman and keeps everything clean. I won't sell her."

I raised the offer to much more than he paid for her, but he still refused.

I found Tychicus and said, "I'm determined to take her to Rome with me. Can you think of any way to help me?"

"That's a real problem," he answered. "She's legally his property, and although slavery is all wrong, you can get into a lot of trouble if you act illegally."

"Well," I said, "I found her and I will take her to Rome."

Tychicus took his mount back to the stable and went to the ship. I rode Pharaoh far out on the desert and let him run. I got back to the ship just before dark, and gave my beautiful red horse a good rubdown before putting him in the stall.

"When do you plan to leave?" I asked the Captain.

"We'll be here two more days," he said. "I plan to leave about midnight of the third day. That will be the highest tide, and we'll need it to reach the open seas since we're so heavily loaded."

"That suits my plans," I told him. "I will have my mother with me just before you sail, but if I happen to be a few minutes late, please don't leave without me."

He was pleased that I had found her. "I won't leave without you," he answered, "but don't bring an officer to my ship."

"I'll be sure that no one follows. No one knows I'm going to Rome or that I'm traveling by ship."

"That's good," he replied. "If no one sees you come here, they'll never think to look here for you."

I obtained a small sheet of papyrus from Tychicus and wrote: *Here is three times the sum you paid for my mother, Hagar. I'm sorry this sale was not voluntary.*

Placing the note and money in a small pouch, I tucked it into my girdle.

After dark the next day I rode to the inn where my mother was and asked for a room.

"I'm sorry, but all the rooms are taken tonight."

I knew he was lying, but I didn't want to start any trouble. "May I speak to my mother for a minute?" I requested.

"I'm sorry but I sent her on an errand, and she won't be back until very late tonight."

I rode slowly down the street until I located another place and obtained a room and a stall for Pharaoh. By the time I ate a quick meal it was very dark. I walked back to the inn where mother was and went to the rear of the building. Taking a position amid some thick bushes about twenty feet from the back door, I watched. Someone lit a candle and placed it on a table. Soon I saw my mother come in to clean the room. I quietly crawled to within a few feet of the open door and waited until the other servant left, and then I stepped to the door and softly called.

She hurried to the door.

"Don't speak, just listen carefully. Tomorrow night, be ready to leave here at eleven o'clock, even if you have to leave without your belongings. Watch for me at this door. When I call, come quickly, all right?"

"Yes, Son," she answered.

"Mother, listen carefully. Take this pouch and hide it somewhere that your master will find it, but he must not find it until you are safely gone."

Without a word she tucked the pouch into her robe and went back to her duties, and I disappeared into the shadows.

The next night at eleven o'clock I walked to the back door and quietly called. Immediately she slid through the door and was by my side.

"Keep very quiet," I whispered as I led her to where I had tied Pharaoh. I mounted, and then helped her up behind me. We rode swiftly in the opposite direction from the ship. We rode for about twenty minutes, using soft places for Pharaoh to leave tracks. I then found a rocky place and left the road. Moving in a great circle, I found a road that I was sure would lead back to the ship. It would take an expert tracker to find our trail, and that would take a lot of time.

The captain ordered the anchor lifted about ten minutes after we were settled on board. I took Mother directly to the room assigned to Tychicus and me, then cared for my horse.

The ship was moving out to sea when I went back to my room. Mother had already gone to sleep.

"I trust that you have done the right thing and no harm will come from it," Tychicus said.

"I'm sure no one saw us come aboard, and I feel I've done the right thing," I replied.

Tychicus pulled a robe across his body and went to sleep. I wrapped in my sheepskin and slept the rest of the night.

We had a pleasant trip. Mother and I, and sometimes Tychicus, walked the decks and talked. As we sailed past the islands, great flocks of birds flitted around, some following the ship for a while.

After talking it over with Tychicus, I asked the captain to set us ashore at a little used port about five miles south of Ostia. I had learned of this port while staying at the inn in Rome.

"I've never done that," the captain said, "but I guess I can. I can't take the ship in close to shore at this point, so I'll send you ashore in the rowboats. Of course," he added, "your horse will have to swim."

We loaded one boat with our camp outfits and Tychicus, and the other with Mother and me. I held Pharaoh's hackamore and he swam behind the boat. The sailors assigned to us had us on shore within thirty minutes.

We rested for a while, and then fastened the outfits on the saddle. I lifted Mother up. Tychicus walked with me as we skirted Rome. We came to Paul's house just before sunrise.

"That was my first horse ride in many years," Mother said as I helped her down.

"How does it feel to be a free woman again?" Tychicus asked.

"Wonderful, Tychicus," she answered as tears filled her eyes, "just wonderful!"

I delivered the letter to Paul from Philemon. He was glad to hear all the good news from the churches at Colosse and Ephesus, and rejoiced with me that I had found my mother.

I told him the whole truth. "Brother Paul," I confessed honestly, "I offered Mother's master three times the price he had paid for her, but he would not take it, so I made the purchase anyway, although I realize it was involuntary on his part." With that, Paul's eyebrow raised and his head tilted while his piercing eyes seemed to be examining my soul.

Though uncomfortable, I continued, "I gave mother a pouch with the money and the note I had written and she hid it where he would find it the next day, after we were well into our voyage."

"I pray that no evil will come of it," Paul said, twisting his lips to one side to hide a faint smile.

In our absence, Epaphras had been tried. He had received ten lashes and was set free. Paul was awaiting our return so he could send Epaphrus to Jerusalem and other churches in Judea with his letters.

Mother was graciously accepted by everyone and took over the duties of housekeeping and cooking.

"But, Mother," I objected, "we are accustomed to caring for ourselves, so I want you to rest for a while."

"I'll rest while I take care of this little house," she replied, "and besides, I'd be miserable if I had nothing to do."

They were all surprised to find that Mother could speak and write the same languages as I. "My father was a very wealthy man who entertained guests from many lands," she explained. "He gave me the best education so I could converse with them."

"It was a shame that you were sold into slavery," Epaphrus said. "That was such a waste of time and talent."

"Perhaps her life was not a waste, Epaphrus," Paul said. "She gave birth to Onesimus and was blessed to serve a master who gave him the chance to study medicine and language. Now he is well prepared to carry the Gospel to others.

"True," I interjected, "but first I must go to Martha." I had thought of her almost constantly since leaving Alexandria, and wondered if they had made good their escape from Rome.

After we were with Paul for five days, he sent Epaphrus to Jerusalem and insisted that Tychicus go with him. "It's much safer to travel together," he explained.

A few days later I got a good deal on a beautiful, strong horse from a man who wanted to move to Egypt.

We fastened our camp outfits and belongings on the saddles. I had purchased several items of clothing for Mother, so I put a few of her things on Pharaoh's saddle, and we rode off to find Martha.

The instructions Abraham had given were very plain. We traveled to a place northeast of Perugia, located in the hills far out of town.

We had an uneventful trip into the Province of Perugia, riding mostly at night and traveling back roads. Though I knew nothing of the country we rode through, I just kept parallel to the Tiber River, asking directions as we passed various shepherds. After we entered the province, we began asking directions to the little town of Gubbio. When we were six or seven miles north of town, we asked a shepherd with whom we spent the night if he knew Abraham and Martha.

"Sure, I know Abraham, and he had a girl with him, but I didn't know her," he replied.

"Do you know where they live?"

"Well," he answered, "I can tell you how to get to the pass, which is a very small opening that enters the mountain country, but I have never gone through it."

"That's wonderful," I said. "Just tell us how to get to the pass and we'll take it from there."

Early the next morning we were in our saddles. Following his directions, we rode due east for about three miles and found the ruins of an old wall, just as he had said we would.

It had been repaired many times for hundreds, maybe thousands of years. The shepherd told us that it was supposed that the Umbrian people had built it hundreds of years before the Romans came.

We rode slowly and watched for two towering rocks that marked the pass. They were called mountains by the natives but did not compare with the mountains I had seen in other countries.

"There are two high rocks," Mother pointed. "Do you think they might be the ones?"

"We'll soon find out," I replied as we headed toward them. The dim trail between the rocks showed recent use. Dismounting, I walked through the pass until I found another trail, leading off to the east. Soon I was back to where I had left Mother. Mounting Pharaoh, we rode through the pass and soon discovered a beautiful country with lots of green grass and running springs. An occasional house dotted the landscape. In the distance I saw a flock of sheep and went in that direction, wanting to ask the shepherd some questions.

"Yes," he replied in answer to me. "Abraham came through here about two months ago. He had a pretty girl with him. He said she was his niece."

"That's him," I replied excitedly, "and that pretty girl is going to be my wife."

"Well, now, I'd say you're a lucky man. I never got married, so I was thinking about courting her myself," taunted the pleasant shepherd who was old enough to be my grandfather. The corners of his eyes crinkled up with a teasing grin. "You've come just in time, Son, otherwise I'd have stole her away."

Following the man's directions, we rode east until we found a creek flowing northeast. Soon we saw a clearing where there were several houses built close together.

"Onesimus!" Abraham had seen us riding up and ran to meet us. "Son, I'm happy to see you. How did things go with Philemon?"

"I'm a free man, Abraham," I replied.

"Thank God. I know Martha will be delighted."

"Uncle Abraham," I said with great pride, "This is Hagar, my mother. God graciously allowed Tychicus and me to find her and bring her with us."

The tremendous joy he felt was expressed as he took both her hands and welcomed her to his home.

Abraham turned to lead us to his house.

Martha ran to meet us and I literally jumped from the saddle. The moment my feet touched the ground, Martha was in my arms.

"I've missed you so much," I said kissing her eager lips.

"Oh, Onesimus," she replied, "you've been on my mind whether awake or asleep."

Mother won their hearts from the very first. Though Martha tried to get her to sit and rest, she pitched in to help with the household chores.

"I've worked all my life," she said, "and I can't be satisfied in idleness."

Martha and I were married about three weeks later when the pastor made his rounds for a few days of ministering to the believers. While he was there, my mother also accepted Jesus Christ as her Savior. We all rejoiced with her in her newfound faith.

Chapter Twelve

Active Ministry

I had agreed to return to Paul after Martha and I had been married for six or eight weeks. I hated to leave Martha and Mother behind, but I was obligated to Paul and to my Lord.

Early one morning, seven weeks after we were married, I rode out, leaving Martha and Mother in tears. I managed to hide mine until I was out of sight.

I stopped in the little town of Gubbio to see if anyone needed my services as a physician, and spent the night there. The next morning I had three patients who came for treatment. The people wanted me to stay, but after treating them, I rode on. I did tell them, however, that I would be returning from time to time and would help them on those occasions. They were pleased, since there was no other doctor in town.

I had a good trip back to Rome. Avoiding the crowds, I tried to keep out of sight of Roman soldiers. They often stopped lone riders who had exceptionally well bred horses, and brought some spurious charge against them. Then they would take their horses.

I arrived at Paul's prison house without incidence.

Luke was also there and it was a pleasure to visit with them both. The apostle Paul was pleased to hear the news from Abraham's camp, and especially glad that Mother had accepted Jesus Christ.

During the three days I spent with Paul, I learned that Demas and Marcus were on a preaching tour in some of the cities of Achaia.

"I told them to visit Corinth on this journey and bring me word concerning its spiritual condition," Paul said.

"I've heard that Corinth is a very wicked city," I remarked.

"It's a political metropolis and the Roman Proconsul resides there," he replied. "It's full of corruption and licentiousness. I preached there for a year and a half some years ago, and worked as a tentmaker, too."

"Tychicus once told me you were a tentmaker," I said.

"I made many fine tents and also sails for ships."

Luke was sitting at his worktable making copies of Paul's epistles. Knowing Paul was in a hurry, he said, "I'll have them ready for Onesimus to deliver to Dalmatia in the morning."

"Thank you, Luke," Paul answered, then said to me, "I don't know what I'd do without Luke. He is a great blessing to me."

While in Rome I bought some medical potions from two of the physicians there. I explained that I was a physician from the north and deemed it a special favor. They were gracious, especially when they learned I was a Roman citizen. I was beginning to lean heavily on my citizenship.

I also saw the Captain with whom we had recently sailed and asked the best way to reach Dalmatia. After a pleasant conversation, he asked with genuine interest, "And how is your mother?"

I'm sure he was remembering our daring escape on his vessel. "She is well and happy," I said and returned his friendly smile.

"I was never quite sure how you pulled that off, and I was nervous until we were well out on the water," he admitted as he gave me a friendly slap on my shoulder.

"Me, too," I said as we laughed together.

The sun was beginning to set when I returned to Paul's prison house.

"These letters," Paul instructed, "are to go to the Province of Dalmatia. Are you acquainted with the area?"

"I only know it lies across the Adriatic Sea from Rome," I answered.

"Do you think you should go by ship or horse?"

After a moment's contemplation I replied, "I talked to a ship's captain this morning, and he said that by the time he could sail south to Syracuse, then turn north to Dalmatia, I could ride a good horse around the northern end of the sea and soon be in whatever city I sought."

"Then God go with you and Pharaoh," he said.

The next morning Paul handed me several scrolls. Each was labeled for a church or an elder in Dalmatia, and wrapped in waterproof skins.

I rode north, following the trail that I used to come to Rome from Abraham's camp. It was a little out of the way, but I would be happy to see my wife again.

I had started a small house before I left for Rome. Abraham, Martha, and Mother had finished one of the rooms which Martha and I took for our bedroom.

"Do you know the country in Dalmatia?" asked Martha as she snuggled against me.

"No, my dear, but I'll find the places to deliver the epistles, and I'll return to you as soon as I can."

"How long do you think you'll be gone this time?"

"I have no way of knowing, but I'll come back by here before going on to Rome."

It required more time to reach Dalmatia than I anticipated. When searching for the pastors and elders, I discovered that persecution was also severe in this area. It was difficult to find the Christians. I had purchased another sword that I kept in sight, due to the many thieves I continually met on the way. This, along with my extra size and big horse made it hard to convince the Christians that I was one of them. It reminded me of Paul's early ministry when the church would not receive him until he had proven himself. Using the sign of the fish, I finally convinced one of them that I was a Christian. After that they welcomed me and gave me information to find the elder. Some of the small Churches did not have regular pastors. They asked me to stay over and preach to them. Knowing that God had called me, I could not refuse.

Two months later I arrived back at Abraham's camp just before dark. Mother had started into the house with a jar of spring water. When she saw me she began to laugh and set the water down in the doorway.

"I didn't spill it this time," she said, giving me a big hug. "I'm glad you're home, Son."

Hearing conversation, Martha came out of the kitchen. Managing to avoid the water jar in the doorway, she ran to me.

"My sweet, precious Martha," I said pulling away from her soft lips. "It seems like a year since I've held you."

As she laid her head on my chest, I noticed Uncle Abraham coming in from the field.

"Onesimus, my boy," he called happily. "I'm glad you're home safely," he said as he hugged me.

I was happy to be back with my family. I explained the many delays I had encountered.

"Well, it's a great blessing that you are able to visit the Christians and preach to them in their own tongue," Abraham said as we sat down to supper.

I was surprised the next morning when seven children came to a little single room schoolhouse that Abraham had built so Mother could teach them. She was so proud of her students, and the parents were just as proud. I knew that no one was more qualified than Mother to teach these little ones.

"Mother," I said, "I'm glad you have a school. It gives you an opportunity to do something for the Lord, but where did these children come from?"

"There are a lot more houses hidden in these hills than it looks like, and two Christian families from Rome have built houses under the north bluff," she answered. "We always have prayer and reading from the law or one of the prophets, and at times we read from one of Apostle Paul's letters. The children love it."

I rested for three days and then went to Gubbio. When the people heard I was there, many came for my services. I treated diseases, set one child's broken leg, and gave herbs and other medication. Some offered small coins, which I accepted, but I also served those who were unable to pay.

The next few days were spent finishing another room on our house.

"I love this place, Onesimus," Martha said. "It is so peaceful, and the people around here are just wonderful."

"I'm glad you like it," I said. "Martha, how would you like to have a little flock of sheep to care for when I'm away on my journeys?"

"Oh, Onesimus," she replied, bouncing up and down. "When can we get them?"

"I bought twenty head yesterday while I was in Gubbio. I'll drive them here tomorrow," I told her. You can graze them on that thick grass south of here."

"Yes, and that's close enough to be in sight of the house while I watch them," she said.

The next day I put the sheep in the well-watered valley about a quarter of a mile from our house. Martha was delighted.

Wonderful news awaited me in Rome. Paul had been given liberty and was waiting my return before going on another missionary journey.

"Onesimus," he said when I walked into the room, "I, too, am a free man, See? I have no chains on my legs, and no Roman soldier to stand guard. Isn't God wonderful?"

"He certainly is," I answered "I know what it's like to be a slave, and I'm sure it is worse to be a prisoner. I know you are very happy."

"Yes, but I'm most pleased because now I can go to Macedonia where I have longed to go for some time," he said. "Then I'll go into Asia, and maybe as Far east as Galatia, if the Lord is willing."

"What do you want me to do now?" I asked.

"I must finish one more letter. It will be ready in a few hours," he said. "I feel that these ministers are in need of help. The letters to the churches will be delivered to Sidon and Seleucia, and those to the pastors will go to Lystra and Lycaonia. I realize I'm asking a great deal from you, as you will have to leave Pharaoh and take ships to the various ports. I'll give you enough gold and silver to pay your fare and have some left over to take care of your wife for a while. Be sure to give Martha and Abraham my love when you see them…oh, yes, and your mother, too."

"Yes, Brother Paul, I will," I assured him. "Then what?"

"The future is yours and God's. Do with it as the Holy Ghost directs you to do," he answered.

"Brother Paul," I said with deep feeling for the great apostle, "I'll never forget the wise teaching and the love you have shown to me."

"Nor will I forget you, Onesimus. You are very dear to me as my brother in Christ and I have confidence in you as a man of God. I expect God will use you greatly," the Apostle said.

"Brother Paul," I said, "I'll ride Pharaoh to Abraham's camp, and then go to the nearest port from there."

"Yes," he replied, "I think that will be best."

While he was finishing the letters, I bought a few things I would need for my journey, and then prepared my pack.

Late that night, the apostle Paul bid me Godspeed. Knowing the danger he was facing, I was overcome with sorrow. This compassionate man of God has become my dearest friend. Will I ever see him again? His ship will sail on high tide at midnight.

I rode out early the next morning.

Tears filled my eyes and I lifted my pen from the papyrus and tried to straighten myself. How can I ever convey in writing, the feelings that I cherish for this mighty warrior for Jesus Christ?

As I laid my pen on the table a drop of rain touched my cheek. It seemed so shockingly cold that I figured my fever was high again. I had been writing while enduring severe pain. The next few days I stayed in our cave, listening to the rain and enjoying the care Martha was showering on me.

"I'm worried, Onesimus," she said with a concerned look. "You're not improving as you should."

"The fever has taken my strength again, and the pain in my right side is almost unbearable at times," I said.

"I can see that, dear," she consoled. "Sarah gathered fresh herbs today and I made tea." She handed me a cup and kissed my forehead. The warm liquid was comforting.

I lay back and listened to my grandson play with his favorite toy, a small lamb that Jacobus had carved for him. I thought about another special friend for whom we named little Tychicus. Brother Tychicus had been there when I needed a friend. He was there for me when I had to go home and face Philemon. I wondered what I would have done had he not been there.

I also thought about my story and smiled as I remembered how wonderful it was to come home from a long journey to the sweet warmth of Martha's lips. Determining to finish it soon, I lapsed into sleep.

Three days later I was writing again, and as always, Martha stayed close to me.

After the Apostle Paul set sail, I rode back to Abraham's camp and spent three days with my family. Martha was delighted with her sheep and had already named each of them.

"Keep Pharaoh staked on some good grass, close to water for a while until he gets used to this place," I instructed Martha. "Then you can let him roam the valley."

"Don't worry about Pharaoh," she said "He'll do just fine."

"He's really a one-man horse," I told her.

"When you return," she said with a mischievous twinkle, "he'll leave you to follow me."

"Martha," I said as she snuggled close, "I'll be gone for several months this time. I'll sail on many seas and travel overland for many miles but I'll come back as soon as I can."

"We'll pray for you daily," Mother said.

The next morning I bade them farewell with an aching heart, and walked across the country to the eastern side of Italy. Then I discovered I'd have to walk another thirty miles to the port. The rocks wore holes in my shoes and my feet burned with multiple blisters, but I finally arrived at the ship I sought. Painfully, I trudged the last few steps up the gangplank, paid my fare, and gratefully found an out-of-the-way spot where I wrapped myself in my old sheepskin and welcomed sleep.

When I awoke it was well into the next day and I was hungry. I ate a big meal in the ship's dining room and wished for home cooking.

I changed ships twice before reaching my first destination. At times I'd have to wait a week or more to get another ship. I suffered much on that trip, traveling through country that was strange to me. Each country had different customs, and to me, most were unknown. Thank goodness I had no trouble with the languages except for one dialect that I found among a tribe that lived to themselves in the hills.

It was eight months before I returned home. Everyone was well, and we all talked and laughed. It was wonderful to be together again. I slept most of the next day.

For a week I roamed the meadows, hand in hand with Martha. We lay side by side on the grassy slopes watching fluffy clouds move across the sky.

One day I said, "What do you think of my going to Gubbio once a week to set up a small practice? Those people really need a doctor."

"Why, I think it's a good idea and I'd like to go with you," she answered enthusiastically.

A few days later Pharaoh pulled Abraham's wagon into Gubbio. He had never been hitched before but did well after a few unsuccessful efforts to get out of the harness.

The town folks were glad to see us, and we stayed three days and treated about forty people.

Martha did some shopping and trading for needed items. I made an agreement with the people to return each month and stay four days. I preached each night in an old empty building and Martha taught them to sing hymns and Psalms that we used in worship at Abraham's camp.

The sheep were doing well. Mother and Martha both enjoyed caring for them. Pharaoh had run of the plush valley and was very much at home there.

In a few weeks we finished building our house and Martha and Mother turned it into a lovely home. I built an extra room to serve as my office, for some of the people had begun to come there to be doctored between my visits to Gubbio. They soon learned that Mother was as good a physician as I, and when I was absent, she cared for their ills.

Abraham's camp was growing. More Christians from Rome and other cities in Italy moved there. Also there were a few from other countries, so we soon had a Christian colony. Mother had over twenty children in her school and both Abraham and I preached to them from time to time.

I lined one wall of my office with shelves for the many scrolls on medicine and the Scriptures I had acquired. I took pride in my practice, both at home and in the little office I had in Gubbio.

I preached in Gubbio almost every time I went, and some of the people who had been idol worshippers had now turned to Christ.

Gubbio was almost twice the size it had been when we first started our practice there, but no Christians had moved there. The town had a priest for the temple of Diana and several other idol gods, and he did all he could to turn the people against Christ and me. The fact that I was their physician caused them to pay little attention to him. The closest physician that I knew of was over a hundred miles away, so they couldn't use him.

In time, God graciously gave us our precious Jacobus. Mother proudly attended at the birth. Jacobus was a healthy infant and he grew fast.

Martha often took little Jacobus with her to watch the sheep and as he got older, he walked beside me as I worked in the garden. I taught him about vegetables and herbs. Martha, Mother, and I spoke in three different languages in our home, and when he was four years old, Jacobus could speak in each of them.

One day I said, "Martha, I've decided to go to Rome and try to find Paul. Maybe I could be of service to him. I am deeply indebted and I want to be available if he needs me."

It was agreed upon and soon I was back on the trail for Rome. I first rode to the old house where Paul had been held prisoner. No one near there had heard a word from him since he left Rome. I found some Christians and questioned them, but they knew nothing. I was about ready to give up and go back home when I met a deacon who told me that he thought Paul was in Nicopolis.

"I really do want to see him again," I said.

"Well," he offered, "If he comes this way I'll send you word. Where can I find you?"

"I practice medicine in a little town called Gubbio, several days ride north of here," I explained. "Just leave word with someone there and they'll get the message to me."

He promised to do so and I turned Pharaoh toward home.

Martha and Jacobus ran to meet me when I rode into the yard.

"What did you bring me from the big city?" asked Martha.

"Well, now, what did you expect?" I teased.

"Jacobus, here is a pair of sandals. They're made of camel's skin and should last until you outgrow them." Though he had never had this type of shoes before, he quickly put them on and ran around the room, telling each of us, "They're made out of a camel!"

"Mother, this is for you." I gave her a coat made of pure white wool.

"Onesimus," she argued, "I know this cost too much. You shouldn't have, but I thank you so much It is beautiful!"

"It will keep you warm this winter," I said and helped her try it on. "It is great with your elegant white hair and it looks stunning on you."

"Uncle Abraham, I bought this for you," I said and handed him a new ax. He had wanted one to cut timber to build another room in his house.

"Onesimus, you are good at knowing just what a man needs," he said, "and I do thank you."

I turned to Martha and asked, "What have you prepared for supper, dear?"

She looked dejected but tried to hide her disappointment by bravely saying, "We have some baked lamb and some of your mother's delicious bread. I'm sure you'll love it."

I could not keep her in suspense any longer. I went to my pack and brought her the biggest package yet.

"This is for my precious wife," I said. She smiled and after flinging her arms around my neck, she proceeded to tear into it, finding three smaller packages. "I knew you wouldn't leave me out, Onesimus."

One package was marked for Mother so she gave it to her. Then she opened another and excitedly slid into a solid black wool coat, a little longer than Mother's. Tears flooded her eyes. "It fits perfectly, Onesimus," she said. "How could you select a coat that fits me so well?"

"Open the other one," I suggested. She did, and out fell thirty yards of the finest material I could find in Rome, some blue, some black, and some a lovely green.

"You and Mother can choose between the black and blue, but I bought the green for you."

"There is enough cloth here to keep us sewing for months," Mother laughed.

I'm not sure why, but that evening has remained in my heart as a very special time in my life. Perhaps it was because I recognized that God had so bountifully blessed us.

I had obtained copies of several of Paul's letters from an elder in Rome, letters I had not seen before, so I set myself the task of making copies to give to the people in Abraham's camp and to the people of Gubbio.

Another year passed. Jacobus was speaking fluent Hebrew, Greek and Latin, but was having a little trouble with Arabic. Mother assured me that she would help him master it in due time. Her school was doing well. She was teaching in Hebrew and Latin since many that were new to the camp spoke a low Latin in their homes. She taught the children to sing songs and hymns that I brought from the churches I visited, and she often made copies for them to take home and teach their parents. Several more families had moved into Abraham's camp and Mother acquired five new students. She taught the girls to cook and make items of clothing.

The sheep were multiplying rapidly, and we would soon have a good income from them.

Some of my patients were able to pay a reasonable fee for my services, but many could not. I welcomed the opportunity to help the poor, considering it to be a work for God.

Chapter Thirteen

The Great Apostle Paul

One day Tychicus rode up. I was thrilled to see him, but his usual smile was absent.

"Greetings in Jesus' name and welcome, Tychicus," I said, though I knew he brought bad news.

He came in and greeted each of us. The women were just placing supper on the table and we were all hungry. Tychicus was unusually silent while we ate. After a while I asked, "What's wrong, Tychicus?"

"Onesimus, I have bad news." he said. "Paul sent me to find you and tell you that he is in prison again in Rome."

I rose from the table. "That's the most evil news I could ever hear, but thank you for telling me. I will go to him first thing in the morning."

I walked outside and stood in the waning light, looking toward Rome, where the best friend I ever had was again in Roman hands—a prisoner for Jesus. I felt a hand on my arm and looked down into Martha's tear-stained face.

"Onesimus," she said, "we both love him so much. I hate being left alone but you must go to him."

"I know, my darling. I'll leave early in the morning."

I went in and spoke to Tychicus.

"Onesimus," he said, "if you'll just wait one day. I'd appreciate it. I rode hard to get here and I know you'll ride hard going back. My horse badly needs a day of rest."

"Of course, Brother Tychicus, we'll wait."

Martha packed my things for another trip. My sheepskin that Philemon bought me when I first went to him was one thing I never traveled without.

We left early on the second day and rode hard, saying little to each other and stopping to speak to no one on the way. We did give the horses a chance to drink and rest once in a while, but we rode until dark. Before daylight, we were in the saddles again.

Paul was in good spirits when we walked into his cold, clammy dungeon cell. This time there was no private prison house. The stench of the dank cave was so bad that it almost took my breath. I could not keep from weeping, as I saw huge rodents running into their holes to escape our invasion. I glanced at Tychicus and saw that tears welled in his eyes.

"I'm the one in chains, Brethren, not you," Paul said lightheartedly.

"But Brother Paul," I said, noticing that his chains had already worn through the skin on one of his ankles, "if I could, I would gladly change places with you."

Paul lifted one eyebrow and tilted his head. "One has already taken my place, Onesimus," he said as a genuine smile lightened his countenance. "When Jesus died on the cross, He took my place. Now I am honored to suffer this small inconvenience for Him."

"I know, but it is a shame that such a one as you should be in this dark and dismal, unholy cell."

"Tell me about yourself," Paul said, changing the subject. "How is your family, Onesimus?"

I talked for over an hour about my work in Gubbio and Abraham's camp. He was delighted to hear about Jacobus, that he was such a talented boy.

"Now, tell me about your arrest," I requested.

"Well, when I was released from prison the last time, I went to Ephesus and ministered there for a while. God did a mighty work in the church. Then I visited Colosse and told them about you and the service you were to me and to the Lord Jesus. Philemon and many others asked me to bring you Christian greetings. Philemon also asked me to tell you that Old Elias passed away, speaking in tongues"

I nodded as wonderful memories flooded my mind. He continued. "From Colosse I went to Heirapolis then to Laodicia, mostly because the caravan I traveled with chose to go there. I didn't want to travel alone. I had sent word for Titus to join me as soon as he could, and he found me at Fair Haven. I organized a church there and left Titus in charge of it. I visited many churches and sent epistles to those I could not see when I was in person. Finally, I went to Troas and spent some time with the church there and stayed in the home of Carpus, who is a good friend of mine."

Paul walked to the table for a drink of dirty-looking water. He paced the floor in silence for several minutes then resumed speaking.

"Forgive me, Brethren," he sat down and leaned toward us, "but I must tell you some sad news. Even as our Lord Jesus Christ was betrayed by one of his own, so I was betrayed by one of our own. He had fallen from grace, and sought the goodwill of the Romans. He told them I was in the home of Carpus and was an enemy of Rome. That night we heard a loud knock on the door and when Carpus opened it, four Roman soldiers came in with drawn swords. They told me I had three minutes to gather the items I wanted to take to prison with me.

"I was kept in jail in Troas for about two months, and then put on a caravan under guard, going to Ephesus. Many of my friends deserted me, fearing that they, too, would be arrested.

"Demas left me, but he had already begun to love this present world more than he loved our Lord. Trophimus went as far as Miletus with me, but he took sick, so I urged him to stay at Miletus and rest. I went on to Ephesus alone." He took a deep breath and then continued.

"I was taken before the Roman Proconsul in Ephesus for trial. It would appear that most of the citizens of Ephesus have gone into a mad frenzy, worshipping the goddess Diana. My preaching repentance and the saving grace of our Lord Jesus Christ angered the priests of Diana. They knew that if the Ephesians became Christians, they could no longer sell their images on almost every corner, or practice their witchcraft for large payments of gold or silver. They tried to have put me to death there, but I appealed to Caesar again, and since I am a freeborn Roman, they had to send me back here to Rome.

"Things really look bad for me this time. The officers who guarded me before are no longer here. The present ones have no regard for me, and they certainly hate Christ. I am treated as any other political prisoner. If I were not a freeborn Roman, I would have been beheaded by now. Hundreds have been martyred since I arrived here."

Paul leaned his shivering body against the cold stone wall, closed his eyes and took another deep breath. He was pale and his voice was shaky. It was obvious that he was weak and spent. "Every day I can look through the metal bars on that small window and see people being beheaded."

"My dear Brother Paul," I said with tears, "is there anything I can do for you, anything at all?"

He was silent for a few moments, and then said, "I have two letters that must be delivered. I hesitate to ask you to do it, but there are few disciples with me now. Most have deserted for fear of persecution. I sent Crescens to Galatia, and Titus to Dalmatia. Luke is still with me and will be coming here later tonight. I'll send Tychicus to Ephesus, for since I was there in prison, there is a greater persecution against the Christians. He will be able to comfort and encourage them."

"Give me the letters and tell me where to take them," I said. "With God's help I will deliver them," I promised.

"Onesimus, I love you greatly. You are my son in the Lord, and a faithful friend," Paul said with deep emotion.

He got up and sipped another drink of water before continuing. "One letter goes to the elders of the church in Phenice, and the other one to the pastors in Fair Haven. I'm sure you know both of these places are on the Isle of Crete."

"Yes," I replied, "and I'll be glad to deliver them for you."

The great Apostle Paul began to weep. "I'm deeply troubled to see God's people suffer such persecution. Jesus said his disciples would suffer in this present world where Satan is worshipped, but God be thanked, Jesus Christ will return in person and put everything right, just as he promised."

"Yes, and that gives me the courage to keep the faith and continue serving the Lord," I told him.

Tychicus had gone to an inn to rest and Paul and I were alone. After a few minutes of silence, Paul said, "Son, I have certain riches of my own from family inheritance and from investments I've made in the past. It's not a great fortune, but it is a goodly sum. I want you to accept it…all of it, and use it in your work as it seems good to you and the Holy Ghost."

"Brother Paul, you've done too much for me already," I protested.

He continued as though I had not spoken. "Use part of it to promote your mother's school, use some in your medical practice, and give to the poor as you see fit."

As I sat thinking about his request, Luke came in. He looked well and I was very happy to see him. We talked for a few minutes while Paul was writing. When Paul finished, he handed me the two letters and a sealed note. "Onesimus, follow these instructions carefully, please."

"No," ordered Paul as I started to break the seal. "Wait until you are on your way to Crete before reading it." I obediently fastened it in my girdle.

The next morning Paul handed me the necessary money for my journey to Crete and back home.

"My son, go with God," he said, clutching my hand with all the love in his heart.

I found it to be one of the saddest moments of my life when I said farewell to the renowned apostle. In stature, he was a small man, but as I placed my hands on his shoulders in a heart-breaking Christian farewell, I realized I was saying goodbye to the largest man I had ever known.

After we prayed I said, "I'll see you when I return."

The Apostle Paul smiled, tilted his head and lifted one eyebrow knowingly, but said nothing.

I had no trouble delivering the letters, and remained on the island for almost four weeks, teaching about Jesus and his Kingdom. I treated many people for diseases that were common to the islands. Most were poor and could pay nothing but love and gratitude.

I had forgotten about the paper Paul had given me and did not read it until I was aboard ship returning to Rome. It was a bill of exchanges drawn on a bank in Tarsus in Cilicia and was sealed with Paul's personal seal. It demanded that I be paid one talent of gold!

That was a staggering amount—fifty times more than I had stolen from Philemon. Immediately I knew that I could not, would not accept it. I would return the bill of exchanges to Paul as soon as I reached Rome.

As I disembarked and started toward the Roman prison, I met a man whom I knew to be a Christian brother. We talked for a few minutes and then he asked me, "Have you heard the news? Tears filled his eyes and his lips began to quiver. With sincere brokenness he said, "Just two weeks ago our great Apostle Paul was beheaded by order of Nero."

Tears began to flow unchecked as my heavy heart ached for this mighty man of God. Alas, I was destined to keep Paul's gift.

Chapter Fourteen

Mission Accomplished

I took Pharaoh from the stable where I had left him when I sailed for Crete, and rode until I found a place where I could be alone. This was the most miserable time of my life and I did not want the heathen idolaters to see me weep. The death of Paul was a great loss to the church and the world. My heart ached. I knew of no other man who could fill the gap where he had stood.

Sleep was far from me that night as I mourned for my noble friend.

The next morning I tried to find Luke, but was told by a Christian friend that Brother Luke had fled the city to avoid an arrest that Nero himself had ordered.

I remember little of the ride home. I seemed to awake from a troubling dream as Pharaoh stopped in our yard and Martha came running toward me.

"What's wrong, Onesimus? Are you ill?"

"I am ill my dear," I said. As I held her, tears ran unashamedly down my cheeks. "Paul is dead. He was beheaded by the order of Nero."

A great lamentation went through Abraham's camp and lasted for many days. I had been able to get copies of various letters that Paul had written. Neighbors crowded our house daily to listen as one of us read them.

After several days, life returned to normal and I remembered the bill of exchange. I called my family together and read it to them.

"I suppose Paul felt he was going to die and wanted you to have the gold," Abraham said.

"I did not intend to accept it…" my voice choked, "but now..."

"What will you do with all that money?" asked Martha.

Paul instructed me to promote Mother's school and my medical profession and to give to the poor.

Mother said, "The school is doing well but there are a few things we could use."

"Yes," Abraham said thoughtfully, "you mentioned just yesterday that you could use more paper, pens, ink, and scrolls."

"Also," I continued, "you could use a larger building so you could have a library."

"Of course," she admitted, "I could use all that."

"And I need a room equipped with beds for patients who are not well enough to travel. They could stay here in our care until they're better," I reasoned.

And, there are many poor people who could certainly use a few pieces of silver to buy food," Martha said.

"It's a long journey to Tarsus," I said. "I'll rest a few days before I begin."

"How will you carry ninety-five pounds of gold?" questioned Abraham. "That's too much, in addition to your weight, even for Pharaoh."

"I'll have to work it out," I answered.

"How long will you be gone?" Martha asked.

"I really don't know," I admitted. "By the time I wait for several ships and all the overland riding, I may be gone for several months."

"Papa," Jacobus asked, "May I go with you?"

"I don't like to say no, Jacobus, but this is a long and dangerous trip. Besides that, you need to stay here and help Uncle Abraham protect the women." Though a little sad, he agreed. Soon I was once again on the road.

I had no trouble getting the gold from the bank in Tarsus. They recognized Paul's signature and seal, and I presented proof of Roman citizenship. That was all that was needed.

"I'll be traveling a long distance by ship," I told the banker, "so please pack the gold in four packs for easy handling."

"Just as you desire, Onesimus," he answered.

I had rented a horse to carry the gold back to the ship in Seleucia, and I placed two packs on each side of the saddle. When my final ship reached port where Pharaoh was stabled, I purchased another horse to carry the gold back home. There were so many thieves and highwaymen on the main roads that I decided to keep to seldom-used trails. At times there were no trails. I met very few people on my return trip but I had plenty of time to talk to God.

After nearly three months, I arrived home in time to celebrate Jacobus' tenth birthday. He was a strong, bright lad, having learned well the lessons Mother taught and was beginning to assume total care of the sheep.

The following year, Mother's health failed and she could no longer teach. Martha kept the school going, but with all her own work, it was difficult.

It was not long before mother died. Sadness filled the camp as she had become very dear to the people who lived around there.

Since the persecution of Christians had lessened in recent years, many families had moved from Abraham's Camp. With little need for a school, Martha discontinued it the next year.

One night about a year after Mother's death, God called Abraham home. He left a void that was never filled, both in our lives and in the lives of his many friends.

Several months later we lost another valuable friend. Pharaoh died. Again, memories of our long rides through several countries and provinces brought joy.

The years sped by and my pastoral work in Gubbio had produced a fine congregation. The new sentiment in that little town for the past several years had been peaceful.

We also enlarged our office in town to provide living quarters for Martha, Jacobus and me. Our flock of sheep had increased and Jacobus moved it to the outskirts of the city. I had given away most of the money that Paul had given me, but God had blessed us with several sources of income and we were independent.

With Martha as my faithful assistant, our medical practice had grown until we could barely handle it.

Jacobus was now twenty-three years old and had married a wonderful girl named Sarah. Over the last year, things had begun to change in Gubbio. The Priests of Diana had again become militant against Christians.

My Christian teaching was causing opposition and hatred to be directed against me by the priests of idolatry in Gubbio. There were now three priests, and they were turning many of the people back to paganism in spite of all we could do.

Jacobus and I spent many hours making copies of Paul's writings, and giving them to the pagans in town. This angered the priests and they incited a mob. Several of …we were stoned...I'm trying to write...I can't recall where...there are so many things to tell, important th...but... I'll...

My name is Jacobus. I sit with my father's pen in hand. My father, Onesimus, is dead. I looked out from the door of our cave yesterday. He was slumped across his table, and papers were scattered on the ground. I took his cold frame in my arms, laid him on the thick grass, and then walked inside. By my expression, Mother and Sarah knew what had happened.

Mother walked calmly to his side. "I've been expecting this, Son, but remember, Paul wrote to the Thessalonians; *Sorrow not, even as others who have no hope.*"

"I remember, Mother," I answered quietly. "I've made enough copies that I'll never forget a word of it."

Tears flowed silently down Sarah's lovely face. "He was the most devoted Christian I've ever known," she said. She picked up little Tychicus and walked away to a large patch of colorful wildflowers where she sat down to cry.

Mother tried to be brave. "Jacobus, bring your Papa's old sheepskin and...." She could say no more but broke into sobs. Though she could not finish telling me, I knew what she wanted.

Going to my father's bed, I picked up the ragged old sheepskin wrap, and went back outside. I dug a grave under the spreading branches of the majestic old tree where he had worked so faithfully through intense pain, in order to tell the world how Jesus Christ can take a sinful life and make it useful.

Sarah and little Tychicus walked back to us, and she handed Mother a beautiful bunch of wildflowers. Tychicus had a bright yellow bloom which he had crushed while holding, but he gave it to his loving grandmother with great pride.

I wrapped my father's cold frame in his beloved sheepskin, and tenderly lowered his frail body, which had once been so powerful, into the ground.

With a simple prayer, we committed his body back to dust. As I lovingly threw the last shovel full of dirt on his grave, I said, "Well, Papa, your story is told. I'll see that it is copied and passed out to many people, and I promise that I'll continue the work that you've so nobly brought thus far."

Sarah picked up Tychicus and then she held my hand. With aching hearts we turned and walked sadly –silently away.

Tears fell profusely as Mother knelt and lovingly placed the colorful bouquet of wildflowers on the fresh mound of loose dirt.

T. Marie Smith

A 'preacher's kid,' Marie lived in several states from Florida to the great northwest.

As one of those individuals blessed with unusual skills, she owned and operated a commercial art studio, served as graphic designer and make-up artist for various TV ministries, and has published poems and short stories. Recently, Marie wrote and published *'Glades Boy*, A Historical Christian Novel, and, with her father, Reverend E. E. COleman, she co-authored a Biblical novel, *Onesimus, The Runaway Slave.*

Marie is an ordained minister, specializing in Chalk-talk Evangelism and also sees her writing as another mthod of spreading the Gospel of Jesus Christ.

She and her husband, Reverend Gene Smith, retired from their pastorate in January 2008, and now enjoy retirement in Southport, Florida.

E.E. Coleman

E.E. Coleman was born June 26, 1908 in Decatur County, Georgia. When he was five years old his family moved to Central Florida where his father worked the logging camps.

At the age of nineteen, Ervin became a Christian and soon entered the ministry.

On June 9, 1931 he married Tonetta Ruby Lee Miller of Fort Myers, Florida. They raised four children, Tonetta Viola, Charles Ervin, Thelma Marie, and William Darrell.

Over his years of ministry, Rev. Coleman served the Church of God as Pastor; Evangelist; Superintendent of Education for the Northwest Bible School in Lemon South Dakota; and Principal for the Spokane Bible School, Spokane Washington. He also taught at the International Bible College in Canada.

Devoting most of his time to research and doctrine, he published many books on Bible Doctrine, a correspondence Bible course, short stories, plays, and has had numerous songs published.

On January 8, 2002, Rev. Coleman was called home to be with the Lord.

We, his family, hope that you will be blessed and inspired as you read *Onesimus.*

www.ingramcontent.com/pod-product-compliance
Ingram Content Group UK Ltd.
Pitfield, Milton Keynes, MK11 3LW, UK
UKHW041943190726
13854UKWH00004B/1769